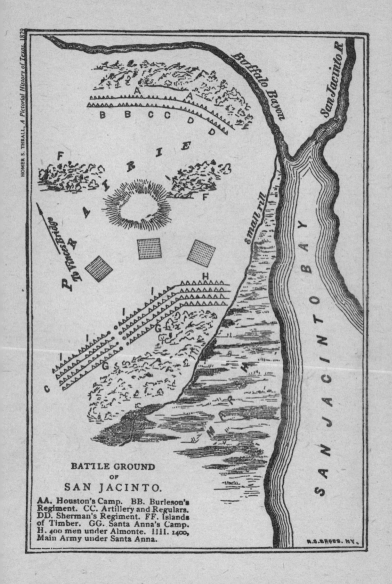

HOMER S. THRALL, *A Pictorial History of Texas, 1879*

BATTLE GROUND

OF

SAN JACINTO.

AA. Houston's Camp. BB. Burleson's
Regiment. CC. Artillery and Regulars.
DD. Sherman's Regiment. FF. Islands
of Timber. GG. Santa Anna's Camp.
H. 400 men under Almonte. IIII. 1400,
Main Army under Santa Anna.

R.S.BROSS. NY.

The Eagle and The Raven

James A. Michener

Drawings by Charles Shaw

TOR

A TOM DOHERTY ASSOCIATES BOOK
NEW YORK

THE EAGLE AND THE RAVEN

Reprinted by arrangement with State House Press

A Tor Book
Published by Tom Doherty Associates, Inc.
49 West 24th Street
New York, NY 10010

Cover art from the painting, "The Surrender of Santa Ana," by William Henry Huddle. Supplied courtesy of the Archives Division of the Texas State Library (Photographed by Eric Beggs).

ISBN: 0-812-51301-0

Library of Congress Catalog Card Number: 90-9684

First Tor edition: April 1991

Printed in the United States of America

0 9 8 7 6 5 4 3 2 1

Acknowledgements

In the original version of this manuscript I had the assistance of two superior secretaries, Debbie Brothers, now the publisher of this book; and Lisa Kaufman, now an editor at Viking Penguin.

Also helping were two fine graduate students, Dr. Jesús de la Teja, now an expert with the Texas General Land Office and Dr. Robert Wooster, now a professor of history at Corpus Christi State University. The work of these four scholars was supervised by John Kings, my long-time assistant.

In the present version of the manuscript I was helped considerably by Dr. Margaret Swett Henson, specialist in Texas history and professor at the University of Houston. Perceptive editorial work was done by Erik J. Mason of Santa Fe, New Mexico, a specialist in Latin American History. The manuscript was read carefully by Jill Mason, a professional editor of Austin, Texas.

Special Thanks
From The Publisher

The publishers would like to extend their appreciation to the following people for their help in the realization of this book: Tom Munnerlyn of State House Press; Bonnie Campbell of the State Preservation Board in Austin; John Anderson of the Texas State Archives; and Ralph L. Elder of the University of Texas Library History Center.

Special thanks to Debbie Brothers, whose creativity, generosity and hard work helped us make a better edition than we could have ever hoped to produce.

Contents

List of Illustrations   xvii

Prologue   1

1. Fledgling Raven   31
2. Eaglet   39
3. The Raven Preens Its Feathers   49
4. The Eagle Bloods Its Claws   61
5. The Raven Topples   83
6. The Eagle Soars   99
7. The Raven Stakes Out Its Territory   113
8. The Eagle Strikes   139
9. San Jacinto—Raven and Eagle at War   155
10. The Eagle Crippled   173
11. Birds of Different Feathers   203

Appendix 1: Letters Mentioned in the Book

Sam Houston to James Prentis, April 20, 1834   213

Sam Houston to James Prentis, April 24, 1834   218

William Travis to the People of Texas and all Americans in the world, February 24, 1836   223

Appendix 2: Chronology   227

Appendix 3: Suggested Reading   229

Illustrations

". . . he irritated them when he appeared in Maryville dressed in Indian garb. . . ."   35

". . . Santa Anna led a wild charge. . . ."   45

"How dare an officer of the United States army appear in this nation's capital in such garb?"   56

"Onto these timbers scores of prisoners were marched and then gunned down by firing squads. . . ."   67

"He marched his men out of Orizaba and joined the rebels. . . ."   74

"With hidden tears . . . she made her parents happy by accepting Houston."   86

". . . he began to call himself the Napoleon of the West and had himself so painted. . . ."   104

"Swinging his cudgel . . . Houston knocked the smaller man to the sidewalk. . . ."   117

The Eagle and the Raven
(The Eagle, Santa Ana, is on the left; the Raven, Sam Houston, is on the right)

The Raven's World, map

The Eagle's World, map

The Battle of San Jacinto, by H. A. McArdle

Courtesy of the Archives Division—Texas State Library; Photographed by Eric Beggs

Portrait of James A. Michener

"... tough-minded local citizens ... drove Cós not only out of Béxar but out of Tejas as well."   135

"When the storm was at its worst ... a horde of Apaches ... began to ravage the stragglers. ..."   148

"... the Texicans rushed after them ... shooting them ... and slashing their throats with long knives."   157

"... Mi General, ha derrotado el Napoleón del Oeste!"   164

"... a solemn procession ... marched ... to the historic cemetery of Santa Paula, where a cenotaph had been erected to the dictator's leg."   180

"The beaded curtain ... parted and an old man of eighty-two ... hopped in on one leg."   196

All art, unless otherwise noted, by Charles Shaw

Prologue

An Old Apple Tree

AN EXPERT ON REGIONAL PUBLISHING TOLD ME that if you omit California, more books about Texas are written, published, and collected than about all the other forty-eight states combined, five times more than even California, also prolific in its published histories. I too can testify that there is a higher percentage of people in Texas who collect books about their state than there is among people up north who collect books about their states like Massachu-

3

setts or Pennsylvania. Texas is a collector's paradise and local publishers know it, for they keep providing a constant flood of books about the Lone Star state.

This book is a curious entry in that pleasant scramble. I admit at the start that it is a hybrid which will be different things to different people. To the publisher, a dear woman of whom I shall speak shortly, it's yet another book about Texas. To the collector it recalls one of the most exciting periods of Texas history, when a firebrand renegade from Tennessee, Sam Houston, emigrated to the Mexican state of Tejas and helped lead the revolution of 1836 which severed the area from Mexico, making it the free sovereign nation of Texas. Sam Houston was opposed by one of the engaging scoundrels of history, Antonio López de Santa Anna, eleven times president of Mexico, four times banished from that nation for life, one-legged but always resurgent. Their duel, even though they meet only once, is the stuff of which captivating history is made. And since this book relates the story of their struggle, it is a modest addition to the Texas bibliography.

To me, the writer, it is not primarily a book about Texas but, rather, it is the last work in a spurt of unusual effort. To explain how this burst of energy came about we must go back nearly eighty years to when I was a country lad. The farmer at the end of our lane had an aging apple tree which had once produced good fruit but had now lost its energy and ability to give us apples. The farmer, on an early spring day I still remember, found eight nails, long and rusty, which he hammered into the trunk of the reluctant tree. Four were knocked in close to the ground, on four different sides of the trunk, four higher up and again well dispersed about the circumference.

That autumn a miracle happened. The tired old tree, having been goaded back to life, produced a bumper crop of red, juicy apples, bigger and better than we had seen before. When I asked how this had happened, the farmer explained: 'Hammerin' in the rusty nails gave it a shock to remind it that its job is to produce apples.'

'Was it important that the nails were rusty?'

'Maybe it made the mineral in the nail easier to digest.'

'Was eight important?'

'If you're goin' to send a message, be sure it's heard.'

'Could you do the same next year?'

'A substantial jolt lasts about ten years.'

'Will you knock in more nails then?'

'By that time we both may be finished,' he said, but I was unable to verify this prediction, for by that time our family had moved away from the lane.

In the 1980s, when I was nearly eighty years old, I had some fairly large rusty nails hammered into my trunk—a quintuple by-pass heart surgery, a new left hip, a dental rebuilding, an attack of permanent vertigo—and like a sensible apple tree I resolved to resume bearing fruit. But before I started my concentrated effort I needed both a rationalization and a guide for the arduous work I planned to do.

As had happened so frequently in my lifetime, I found the intellectual and emotional guidance I needed, not in the Bible, into which I dipped regularly, but rather in the great English poems on which I had been reared and many of which I had memorized. I was particularly impressed by the relevancy of the opening lines of that splendid sonnet which young John Keats had penned when he feared, with good cause as events proved, that he might die prematurely; he died at age twenty-six:

When I have fears that I may cease
    to be
Before my pen has gleaned my teeming brain,
Before high-piled books, in charactery,
Hold like rich garners the full-ripened
    grain . . .

How apt those words seemed, more so those of the second line than the first, for I was not so much concerned with death as with my unwritten works. I had on file in the back recesses of my memory such a wealth of enticing subjects about which I would like to write that my brain could justly be termed teeming, and I regretted that my typewriter would never be able to glean them all. I was almost eighty years old. Since it took me about three years to write a long work, if I had thirty viable subjects the task would require ninety years. That would make me one hundred and seventy when I finished, and I could not recall many writers who continued working so long, not even the doughty ancients in the Old Testament. Much of what I would like to do would have to be left unfinished.

The last two lines of the segment touched me deeply. Keats did not want to stop writing before he had piled up his quota of books, filled with whatever rich garners of ideas and images he had amassed. Like the poet, an idol of mine, I had some books I desperately desired to finish.

I knew what my ambitions were, but what of my capacity to fulfill them? Fortunately, I had in my teens memorized those powerful lines composed by John Milton when, in mid-life, he was struck blind. I had recited them to myself a thousand times, and now they rushed back to give me the kind of strength that he had found:

When I consider how my light is spent,
Ere half my days, in this dark world and
   wide,
And that one Talent which is death to hide,
Lodged with me useless, though my Soul
   more bent
To serve therewith my Maker, and present,
My true account, lest he returning chide . . .

That ringing challenge, that determination to 'present my true account,' had defined the goal of my writing, so firmly grounded that it had become a permanent ambition. At the tragedy of Kent State I had endeavored to render an unbiased account of the killings, in South Africa an honest report of the racial injustices, in Israel the deadly duel between religions, in Hungary the unembellished facts about the revolution, and in Poland a factual account of that nation's long struggle.

Any explanation for my prolific output these last four years thus relies upon the precept of Keats, whom I think of as a gifted friend pondering his future, and upon the stern admonition of Milton, whom I regard as a mentor, encouraging me to give 'a true account.' Much of what I am about to say will sound improbable or even preposterous, but it is true. It can best be considered a hesitant *Apologia pro Vita Mea*, and I hope it will be so received.

Between the years 1986 and 1990 I would write ten books, publish seven of them including two very long ones, and have the other three completed in their third revisions and awaiting publication. It was an almost indecent display of frenzied industry, but it was carried out slowly, carefully, each morning at the typewriter, each afternoon at exciting research or quiet reflection.

I began with the harshest test of all. From the earliest days of my writing I had wanted to contrast the tropical scenes I had utilized in

Tales of the South Pacific with the bleak land-
scapes of the North Pacific, more especially its
Arctic reaches. In my forties, fifties and sixties
I had been wary of my ability to withstand the
climate north of the Arctic Circle, where much
of my novel would have to be located, but now
at nearly eighty I thought: 'If I'm ever going to
do it, now's the time to try.' On the shortest
day of the year, 21 December, when Arctic
nights are longest and coldest, I flew to Fort
Yukon and spent several days at minus 52 degrees Fahrenheit, then on to Eagle and Point
Barrow, where the cold deepened. I found that
I liked it, for there were ways to protect myself.

In the spring of 1987 the novel was finished
and ready to submit to Random House, my
longtime publisher, but at that unpropitious
moment the editor on whom I had relied for
three decades was incapacitated by his own
medical problems, making his editorial work
impossible. So *Alaska*, which should have appeared in print much earlier, was postponed,
with my full approval, until late 1988.

As a professional writer I could not spend
unexpected free time in idleness; for me that
would have been impossible. So I moved to
Miami and plunged immediately into the research for a long novel on the Caribbean, an
area I had known well in times past. But as I
started work in the fine library at the University of Miami, a major newspaper, in antici-
pation of the two hundredth anniversary of
the writing of our national Constitution to be

celebrated in 1989, invited me to write an essay on that historic event to which the paper would devote an entire issue of one of its Sunday sections. The idea was most appealing, for I had done a good deal of research on that miraculous summer of 1787 when the thirty-nine delegates met in Philadelphia to draft the document that secured our liberties and served our nation so admirably. I had written about the event before but, of greater interest, a major musical group had once asked me to write a cantata about the Constitution, the music to be composed by a distinguished American musician. The idea had come to nothing, but the extensive work I had done in preparation still echoed in my mind.

So I was receptive when the newspaper suggested the essay, and I stopped my Caribbean work to engage in this patriotic venture for which I had unknowingly prepared myself. I wrote the essay, polished it and mailed it in, but after reading it the editors said: 'Your ideas are so attractive it seems to us they'd be more effective if expressed in dramatic form. Could you convert them into a novel?'

The suggestion was practical. Events surrounding the Constitution as I now perceived them were exceedingly dramatic and I worked diligently to redraft my essay, telling its story through the lives of one family to whom it had been especially significant. I was happy with the transformation and proud when I mailed it in. To me at least, the story sang of the American experience.

While I was in the hospital for a major operation, the editors informed me: 'We've changed our minds. We don't like the story form. We see it now as an essay. If you care to redraft it, we'll reconsider.' I did not answer the message. From my bed I growled: 'I rewrote it as a novel. I'll publish it that way,' and I did. As *Legacy* it was well received and was picked up by various foreign publishers.

Returning to my novel on the Caribbean I felt refreshed by the interruption, but as my research and writing approached an end I found myself forestalled by international events which proved so frustrating that I wondered if I could ever finish the task. I needed to visit Cuba to complete my research, but could not get a visa. When Castro took his island into the arms of communist Russia, the United States imposed a strict embargo on trade and travel with Cuba. American citizens were forbidden to visit the island, lest they leave behind the dollars needed by Castro for his faltering economy. As a private citizen I was forbidden by our government to go, and as a writer who might report unfavorably on Cuba, Castro would not allow me to come. My work ground to a halt.

One evening, as I walked the streets of Miami in frustration, I recalled a chapter written for my novel *Alaska*, a piece of writing I had liked when composing it and had continued to like—unfortunately, my editors did not. They were correct in their judgment, for the long section dealt primarily with Canada's gold rush and not Alaska's. When they advised cutting I saw the justification for it and promptly agreed.

But a strong piece of writing does not die easily, and if the author's emotions are entangled, its life goes on. The more clearly I remembered the Canadian portion of my manuscript the more attached to it I became, and one day I telephoned a Canadian publisher whom I had never met and about whom I knew nothing: 'Would you consider publishing, as a short Canadian novel, a very strong segment I had to cut from my *Alaska* manuscript?'

'I'd have to see it.'

'I'll mail it.'

The book, much improved from what it had been when part of the larger novel, was published in Canada in the autumn of 1988 and in an American edition in the spring of 1989. To my surprise, and everyone else's, *Journey* became a book club selection and a work well-received in Canada, the United States, and Great Britain, was later published in some dozen foreign editions, and may become one of my best-remembered works. A book that had been dead was reborn.

Free again to return to my Caribbean manuscript, a fortuitous event occurred to end my frustration with it. Both the American and Cuban governments finally decided that I could fulfill my long-felt desire: I would be allowed to visit Cuba to round off my researches on the Caribbean. It had taken me three tedious years to engineer this permission.

The Gordian knot was cut, and I was allowed six exciting days in those parts of Havana about which I wished to write, plus a visit of homage to Ernest Hemingway's *finca*, maintained in fine order as a national monument by the Cuban government. My editorial assistant who accompanied me, John Kings, took his camera with him and captured over a hundred artistic and revealing color photographs of contemporary Havana, a noble city much depleted by communist neglect and the American embargo which had seriously incapacitated the entire country.

When Kings and I returned to the States, numerous people who heard my stories and saw Kings' pictures said: 'That ought to be a book.' In time word reached Jack Kyle, the imaginative director of the University of Texas Press, who within days decided to publish. To his delight and my amazement, the resulting work evolved into a handsome publication.

Although this was astonishing we had no great hopes for the book, but we had not counted upon the intense interest readers would have in off-limits Cuba, nor the many travelers who remembered Havana in its days of glory. To our surprise, an extra printing was required, a book club took it as an alternate, and foreign publishers snapped it up. It illustrates what good things can happen to a book written with vigor and published with care. It was an accident, the kind of adventitious good luck that cannot be anticipated.

A change of editors at my major publisher, engineered by him, not me, meant that publication of my finished novel *Caribbean* had to be delayed. In this hiatus, again finding myself with free writing time, I assembled thoughts which had been ripening throughout the decades as hesitant beginnings of an autobiography. Under self-generated pressure I wrote fourteen chapters of a new kind of biography, the first seven chapters describing me as if I had never written a word, the last seven as if I had done nothing else. It provided an unemotional picture of a professional writer at work.

When that was rewritten and edited, I put it aside and turned to a short novel which I had long wanted to write. It consisted of only four chapters, each focusing upon a different character involved in the writing and publishing of a novel: the writer, the editor, the critic, the reader. The setting for the story is my homeland, the Pennsylvania Dutch country. When it had been redone three times with radical changes it, too, was placed on the shelf to await future publication.

Now a most curious event intruded. In this book about the writing of an imaginary novel, I had years earlier devised the basic plot line of the third chapter, involving the managerial shakeup of the publishing company with which the fictional writer and editor have long been associated. This American company is acquired by an American conglomerate which deemed it prestigious to own a publishing company whose writers were well known and whose books attained prominence. But, as often happens in the book industry, the financial managers of the conglomerate quickly learn publishing is not a go-go industry producing twenty and thirty percent profits each year—eight percent is closer to fact.

Disgusted with the lackluster financial performance of their publishing house, my imaginary corporate managers decide to sell it to anyone who will take it off their hands and, in a shameful peddling of a great company from one marketplace to the next, they finally manage to pass it off to an imaginary German cartel.

My secretary's notes, typed out and dated, affirm that I wrote this long passage well before 3 May 1989, finished revising it in September, cranked in the final corrections on the floppy disk of our word processor and, by 20 October, had my imaginary company safely sold to the imaginary Germans.

Three weeks after completing the chapter and having it typed in final copy, I was on a cruise ship in the Caribbean, quietly celebrating the publication of my novel on that enchanting body of water, when the purser brought me a long telex from New York. It advised me that the longtime head of *my* real publisher, Random House, had either been fired by the head of *his* conglomerate or had retired under pressure. His place was to be taken by a gentleman from another nation who had learned publishing by working for one of the German conglomerates. Thus fact, as it so often does, imitated fiction, this time within three weeks.

This rupture of my publisher's structure left me with two finished manuscripts on my hands. Also at this moment my copy editor of thirty-five years, a brilliant woman who had mastered the nuances of the English language and who had been my powerful guide, retired from the company, depriving me of any long-time associates there. The two manuscripts gathered dust in my files, work completed but without a home.

While these affairs were unfolding, one of those events which make writing emotionally rewarding was transpiring. The Polish government, which had banned my novel *Poland* with harsh words, since it spoke poorly of communism, had furthermore let me know I would never again be welcomed in that country, a decision which grieved me. Now, with *glasnost* in the air, the government reversed itself, slipping me word that if I wished I would be allowed back to meet with old friends in the Warsaw Writers Union—men and women who had survived harsh burdens and for whom I had profound respect. I flew immediately to Poland.

When I arrived, a surprise awaited me, for I was first taken not to the hotel at which I had reservations but to the guest house reserved for visiting dignitaries. On a sleety November night reminiscent of the Poland I had known so well, I was taken to the building in which the writers met, but when we reached there we did not stop. The car proceeded to famous Warsaw Castle, where I was hurried underground to the cloak room and then upstairs to the huge gold-and-silver ballroom reserved for meetings with heads of state. As I entered the salon I found awaiting me some five hundred of Poland's leaders in various fields, with the prime minister of the nation striding forward to greet me and pin upon my left chest Poland's highest civilian decoration. The leaders still did not like what I had said about communism, but they realized that I had written about their nation with affection and honesty and that my novel had circulated world wide, bringing much favorable attention to their land and to the heroism of the stubborn people who occupy it. With my pen I had made myself an honorary Pole, and I reveled in the distinction.

From Warsaw I flew to Rome to pay my respects to an old friend, Pope John Paul II, whom I had known years ago in Krakow as Karol, Cardinal Wojtyla, and with whom I had later worked in a television show about Polish culture. When he ascended to the papacy, the only extant television footage of him available in English was a long interview I'd had with him in his Krakow garden.

Now I was to have dinner with him as we discussed old memories and recent events. It was a nostalgic reunion strengthened by collateral visits to the churches of Rome, meetings with old friends in the Catholic hierarchy, and a renewal of my longtime association with our two United States ambassadors in Rome, Maxwell Raab, our veteran ambassador to Italy, and Frank Shakespeare, our skilled ambassador to the Vatican.

Events surrounding these two visits, to Warsaw and Rome, were so colorful and the photographs that depicted the pilgrimages so evocative that when we arrived back home, Polish enthusiasts who had been gratified and excited by the warming relationships with Poland and the vision of their Pope installed in the Vatican, suggested that a short book celebrating the two events be published privately and distributed to the Polish community in America.

Intrigued by this idea, I applied myself to the drafting of a manuscript summarizing the pilgrimage. When it was finished the Rodale Press near my home, distributor of the world's best thesaurus, the *Rodale Synonym Finder*, decided that the manuscript and its accompanying photographs merited traditional publication, and editorial work started. The spontaneous situation which had resulted in the Cuba book had been duplicated.

Several weeks after I moved back from the University of Miami to my home base at the University of Texas, a most enticing invitation arrived. A major publisher was in the process of bringing out a series of children's books, beautifully illustrated by artists well known for their work in imaginative illustration. This series would focus on famous dramatic works, each story narrated by someone closely related to the stage show being featured. Thus Dame Margot Fonteyn would tell the story of *Swan Lake*, which she had danced, and Leontyne Price that of *Aida*, which she had sung. Since each had portrayed the heroine of her tale many times, the results were charming and the illustrations vibrant.

The editors had hit upon the interesting idea of inviting me to tell the abbreviated story of *South Pacific*, the musical drama in the series, and I leaped at the opportunity, for the story of that Broadway triumph was a tale worth telling. The task of writing a children's book was far more difficult than I had imagined, because space was limited and vocabulary had to be scaled to young readers, but it was enjoyable to listen again to the old record of Mary Martin and Ezio Pinza singing of their enchanted evenings. At the completion of the children's part of the book I was asked to relate briefly the circumstances under which the play came about, and this allowed me to pay tribute to that talented group who had made the musical possible—poet Oscar Hammerstein, musician Richard Rodgers, dramatist Josh Logan, financial wizard Leland Hayward, and the incomparable cast. Rarely have I experienced more pleasure in writing than during the Christmas when I wrestled with this apparently simple children's tale.

While I was working long hours every day on this tangle of obligations, nine books finished to one degree or another, an almost ridiculous event intruded. Back in Texas I had lunch one day with Debbie Brothers, a remarkable young woman who had been my helper seven years earlier during the writing and publishing of my novel *Texas*. I remembered her as a beautiful, corn-fed Nebraska farm girl with a rowdy wit and an extraordinary capacity for hard work. She had proved most helpful and I regarded her with affection.

The adjective *remarkable* did apply to her, for as she worked with me in those early years I noticed that she was paying close attention to all facts relating to my profession. She loved books and could not learn enough about them; at times I feared she was spending rather more effort on my work than facts or salary warranted. I was pleased to see that she absorbed immediately anything I told her. Even though she had a college degree, it was her native good sense that made her so exceptional and I wanted to help her learn.

I'd had great good luck with my secretaries. In early days at Macmillan in New York the young women who worked with me—six Smith College graduates in a row—quickly graduated from my tutelage to good positions in publishing. In later years two assistants had achieved exceptionally good positions, Leslie Laird from Vanderbilt becoming an editor at a succession of posts, and Lisa Kaufman of Wesleyan a full-fledged editor at two different New York houses. Two male assistants had done equally well: Jesús de la Teja, as an editor and writer for the state government of Texas, Robert Wooster impressively successful with his academic writing. While still working with me Robert landed an assignment to do a major book on the military outposts of nineteenth-century Texas, had his doctoral thesis on army conditions in the old west accepted by Yale University Press, and received invitations from other presses to write for them. He was on his way to a brilliant career.

But Debbie Brothers had provided the biggest surprise. One day she came rather apologetically to my desk with a present. In a low voice she said: 'Watching you, Mr. Michener, I've decided to become a publisher,' and she handed me a handsomely printed book dealing with a little-remembered niche of Texas history. As I admired it, she handed me another, the first two volumes in a publishing venture in which she was a partner, State House Press.

As I studied the two books I thought: This can't be. A young woman with no background for the task cannot say to herself: 'I am going to be a publisher,' proclaim herself as such, and proceed to publish books. But there they were, two of them, and fine looking, too.

Before I left Texas for my writing job in Alaska, Miss Debbie was a full-fledged publisher, printing editions of 3,000 copies, selling them all, and going back to press with those that did especially well. While I was absent from the state I lost track of her operations, but I had the impression she had published some fifty reprints dealing with Texas history.

At our lunch when I asked Debbie how her press was doing she gave a glowing account. Then she hesitated and looked at me in the way she had when wanting to know something about the publishing world: 'Mr. Michener, when I typed some of the late corrections on your novel *Texas* there was a chapter which you had cut out of the story, Chapter Four I think it was.'

I could not remember that distant event, for I had written the original version of the chapter years before, but when she gave me the title of the long-dead chapter it sprang to life: 'You called it "The Eagle and The Raven." Exciting comparisons of the adversary generals, Santa Anna and Sam Houston.'

'Yes! I spent a lot of time on that chapter, but nobody else felt it should be included in the book, and for good reason. It was written outside the normal story-telling pattern. More historical than narrative. I hated to cut it, but had to.'

I put down my fork, leaned back, and recalled those days. I had wanted to contrast the archetypal Mexican and Texan, two charismatic men, each flawed in so many ways yet dominant figures in their two nations, Mexico and Texas. I had read six or seven biographies or studies of each, had traced their movements in Mexico and Texas and refought the battles they conducted. Santa Anna had won all the early battles against the Texicans, as they called themselves at that time, especially the crucial battles of the Alamo, where he slaughtered all the Texicans, and at Goliad, where he even more hideously murdered hundreds of Texicans who had honorably surrendered into his protection. But stubborn old Houston had adopted the historic tactics of the Roman general Quintus Fabius Maximus, who defeated the Carthaginian Hannibal by running away from him until Hannibal's men were exhausted and the terrain favorable to the Romans. Then Fabius stood firm, defeated the Carthaginians, and won himself a place in the world's dictionaries: *Fabian tactics: avoidance of direct confrontation in order to gain the advantage and the victory*. At the climactic battle of San Jacinto, on 21 April 1836, Sam Houston stood firm, won the victory, captured Santa Anna and helped establish the Republic of Texas.

In their later years each leader fell into disrepute in his own land but after death lived on as an icon of his nation: Houston a cherished symbol fondly remembered, Santa Anna neither cherished nor fondly remembered but a symbol, nonetheless, of one of the most important eras of Mexico's history. Since I had originally felt this to be a story worth retelling, and preserving when retold, I became attentive to Debbie's suggestion that she be allowed to print it, telling her: 'If you could get our old friend Charles Shaw to do a dozen of his great illustrations of Texas history, perhaps portraits of the two generals, one with an eagle, the other with a raven, we might have a fine bit of Texas bookmaking that local collectors would want to keep.' The deal was struck, and I believe I was happier about it than she.

I have taken the trouble to bring this book into print and to write of its genesis in this highly personal way for a respectable reason. Like the old apple tree into which the rusty nails had been driven, I have had a burst of energy I could never have anticipated, not only to write more books but particularly to leave a picture of a professional writer at work. Everything I have done in this fruitful period of my early eighties has had but one ambition: to give a true account of myself as a writer who has developed and practiced a unique style of writing. I tackled the very difficult Alaskan book at an advanced age when it seemed improbable that I could withstand the rigors of an Arctic winter. I moved on to the Caribbean book, whose research entailed nearly a dozen extended trips to remote corners of that sea and to difficult locations like Cartagena and Portobello. I successfully fought to get into Cuba and back into Poland.

More relevant, as in *Journey* in which I appended a long note explaining the birth, death, and resuscitation of that manuscript showing how a writer defended his work, and as in the book about my pilgrimage to Poland and Rome in which I did much the same, in this prologue I am again describing how a chapter of a book, once rejected because it was inappropriate in a specific context, can achieve life in another. Viewed as a whole, this mix of long books and shorter excerpts does create a glimpse of a writer at work.

Curiously, during this spurt of energy I never thought of myself as either compulsive or driven. Nor am I. Through decades of writing I have acquired certain patterns of behavior and workmanship which have enabled me to write long books. I merely adhere to those solid rules. I rise each day at seven-thirty, wash my face in cold water but do not shave, eat a frugal breakfast of bran sprinkled with banana, raisins, and skim milk—no sugar—and go directly to my desk, where the day's work has been laid out the night before.

With delight and a feeling of well-being, I leap into whatever task awaits and remain at it until half after noon, when I have a light lunch after which I take a nap. I never compose in the afternoon but do research and meet classes at the university. At dusk each day, regardless of the weather, I take a mile walk at a rather brisk clip. Supper, the evening news, a nine o'clock movie if a good one is available on television, a half-hour of cleaning up my desk at eleven, and off to bed.

Each day, without fail, I find time to listen to classical music on my new compact disc player, a marvel of these times, with cartridges into which I can load six of the miraculous silver circles, each giving an hour of almost perfect sound reproduction. Into one cartridge I place the piano music of Chopin, Beethoven, and Liszt. In another, six of my perennial favorites: The Schubert *Octet*, the Bartok *Concerto for Orchestra*, the Brahms *First*, the Beethoven *Ninth*, the Stravinsky *Rite of Spring* and *Petrouchka*. In a third, six wonderful discs of the great operatic arias, some by Caruso and his peers in the 1920s, some by the current stars.

A feature of each cartridge of six discs is that its selections of fifty or sixty separate bits of music can be played in random order, always different as the computer determines, thus providing me with a varied and exciting concert. I never play the music while I work at original composition but often listen to it when doing routine work like checking pagination, reading stacks of accumulated mail, or filing research material. The long walks, the sensible diet, and the music keep me healthy and able to complete the work.

Because I adhere to such patterns, I find it appropriate that the subject matter of this book should involve two men who also liked to tackle varied problems and who followed their own arcane rules of behavior. In the case of General-President Santa Anna the comparison is especially relevant for he also lived into his eighties, as ornery and feisty as I try to be.

I find a special pleasure in bringing this excised segment back to life, because doing so enables me to include in the final pages two incredible real-life illustrations of Santa Anna in his most preposterous behavior: the apotheosis of the leg he lost in battle, and his brazen attempt in his near-blind eighties to engineer one final, majestic hoax on the Americans whom he had flimflammed so often before.

One nagging question remains. Did the old tree get back to work producing apples only because the shock of the rusty nails reminded it of death? By analogy, did I labor so diligently because of my age and the approach of a time when I could work no more? Was I, like Keats at twenty-six, apprehensive of work-ending death?

I think not. I write at eighty-three for the same reasons that impelled me to write at forty-three: I was born with a passionate desire to communicate, to organize experience, to tell tales that dramatize the adventures which listeners might have had. I have been that ancient man who sat by the campfire at night and regaled the hunters with imaginative accounts of their prowess that morning in tracking down their prey. The job of an apple tree is to bear apples. The job of a storyteller is to tell stories, and I have concentrated on that obligation.

The Eagle and The Raven

Chapter 1

Fledgling Raven

 IT WAS AS IF TWO POWERFUL BIRDS HAD entered the sky within a single year, The Eagle in the south, The Raven in the north, each circling and gaining strength, each progressing in the consolidation of its own powers. For forty-two tempestuous years the adversaries would fly in ever-widening orbits until confrontation became inevitable. They would meet only once, a clash of eighteen culminating minutes in the spring of 1836 which would change the history of the world.

This account of those forty-two years of preparation kaleidoscopes their wild flight through the histories of the United States and Texas.

The Raven, so called by his closest friends and many of his enemies, was born first, on

31

2 March 1793, to a Scots-Irish family which had settled in Rockbridge County of western Virginia. Sam Houston was one of nine children, a difficult lad who would accept only a few terms of schooling, but who did acquire an intense love of reading books of high quality. Even before the age of ten he showed that he was going to grow up to be a large man and a stubborn one, never afraid to act on his own or to explore the remote reaches of the Blue Ridge Valley beyond Lexington, the county seat.

In 1807, when Sam was fourteen, his father died while planning a removal from Virginia to the more inviting land of Tennessee. After the burial, Sam's resolute mother loaded her many children into two wagons and started down the valley roads that would carry them to their new home. For much of the way Sam managed the new five-horse wagon, guiding it past Roanoke and Bristol and into the mountainous country of eastern Tennessee.

There the Houstons started the long, rough ride over barely sustained roads to Knoxville, the capital of the new state, but they did not linger among its log houses. Widow Houston preferred rural life and kept her family heading south to the insignificant town of Maryville, a chain of rude log huts strung out along both sides of a rutted road.

Here, at the edge of a wilderness which would rapidly become a rich agricultural area, the Houstons could have halted and shared in the prosperity that would soon mark the county seat. Instead they forged on, ten miles farther into the roadless forest where, on the banks of two streams, they settled on some four hundred promising acres. Cutting out fields for crops and a space for their new house was laborious work, and even though the Houstons managed to buy slaves to do the heavier tasks, the six boys had to labor strenuously.

During this early period Sam displayed three characteristics that would mark his life: he did not like tasks he considered routine, he was strongly inclined toward a military life, and he had a most peculiar and pronounced affinity for the Indians who were being driven from their ancestral lands. His aversion to work was easily indulged; he turned jobs over to his five brothers. He also became adept in woodsmanship, with a curious affection for whittling, a skill he would practice for the rest of his life.

His delight in military matters was demonstrated in the skills he developed with rifle and sword, and by the age of sixteen he was an accomplished frontiersman thirsting for adventure. From his father he acquired several habits that remained with him. The senior Houston had been an ardent militiaman in the American Revolution, and Sam inherited this love of battle. His father also had the habit of moving away from where he was living whenever life there became complicated or boring. Sam too became a fighting, wandering man.

Laziness and a desire to fight were understood in Tennessee, especially if the growing lad was the size of a young ox with power to match, but his preference for life with Indians could be neither explained nor condoned. One day, to the astonishment of all, Sam simply left home and traveled alone on foot across the streams and mountains of Tennessee to make his home with the Cherokees. This Indian nation was among the noblest of America's native tribes, but had been forced to move under increasing pressure from the white men, to locations west of the Tennessee River.

He lived with them a year, learning their language and their ways, then returned to Maryville without telling anyone where he had been or what he had been doing. After another brief and restless try at Tennessee society, at age seventeen he was charged with riotous behavior, disturbing the peace, and preventing the local sheriff from performing his duties. He was fined five dollars at Blount County Court and warned against further offenses threatening the state. He appears to have been in uniform at the time of this tempestuous behavior, a member of the militia, and it is clear from what his colleagues said of him that he was already regarded as a potential leader of men.

He might have started his military career at that point but, disgusted with civilization after his brush with the law, he instead returned to his Indian friends. This time he spent nearly

two years with them, perfecting his knowledge of a way of life which he admired and with which he was content, and receiving from them the honored name of The Raven. He carried with him a copy of Pope's translation of the *Iliad* and, in later years when he had attained a measure of grandeur, often reflected that what he prized most of all were those early times when he read Homer in the wilderness and wandered the mountain streams with the young Indian women who became his intimate companions.

Here in the wilds of western Tennessee he acquired the Indian's love of rhetoric, his appreciation of nature, his sense of high honor, and his willingness to fight in defense of his prerogatives. He also accumulated a hundred-dollar debt from buying liberal gifts for his Indian friends, male and female. Sam Houston's life constitutes a grand mystery, indeed a chain of almost insoluble mysteries, which cannot be solved or even investigated without remembering that here was a tough-minded Scots-Irishman, steeped in Homer, who chose at three important intervals in his life to cast his lot with the Indians. He was thus one of the quintessential Americans, for he combined in a massive body and an able brain two of the major strains of our national history: the rigorous frontiersman and the natural Indian.

We leave Houston in the year 1812, at the age of nineteen, a reckless wanderer among the tribes, a failed scholar, an insubordinate militiaman, and a youth apparently unfitted for civilian life. He was about six-feet-four, some said six-six, weight just under two hundred pounds, a crack shot, a good horseman, a reciter of poetry and, like his mother, a believer in the Bible. His neighbors considered him the least of the Houston sons; he irritated them when he appeared in Maryville dressed in Indian garb: moccasins, long hair adorned with a feather, deerskin pants, and covering all a bright red-and-blue blanket pulled close about his broad shoulders.

If anyone in those years had predicted that young Sam Houston, a squaw man trading among Indians in Arkansas, would become in succession a congressman in Washington, a governor of Tennessee, the president of a new nation and then a United States Senator with a chance of becoming president, he would have been jeered.

Chapter 2

Eaglet

 ON 21 FEBRUARY 1794, ELEVEN months after the birth of Sam Houston in Virginia, a minor mortgage broker named López, who worked in the Mexican gulf port of Veracruz, hurried northwestward to the mountain town of Jalapa, called Xalapa in official documents, where a son was being born.

Veracruz was Mexico's most important seaport and the source, because of customs collected there, of much of its wealth. During the frequent revolutions that swept the country, whichever contesting power controlled the port also controlled the treasury. It was a steaming little city, one of the unhealthiest on earth, with regular plagues killing thousands each summer and *el vómito*, yellow fever, attacking the rest of the time.

But the city had an unquestionable charm, its stout white walls promising a safety which rarely materialized, its plazas attractive with their sturdy church facades, and its waterfront a favorite walking place, especially when breezes blew in from the sea. It provided some of the best food in the country: excellent beef from the nearby ranches, fruits of unequaled richness and variety, and all kinds of succulent seafood. It was a tropical city, with great jungles reaching almost to its gates, and it was also exciting, for here the ships docked after their journey across the Atlantic, bringing news of Spain and Cuba.

The streets of Veracruz were narrow, lined with tropical trees and overlooked by windows protected with handsome iron grills. The walls of the houses were mostly white, giving the city a look of cleanliness it did not merit. Occasionally some daring owner, usually one newly rich, would paint his house a soft blue or pink, lending a dancing color to the place.

Several buildings predominated: the cathedral, the stout customs sheds along the waterfront, the arsenal where the troops lived, but above all the gaunt fortress stuck on an island in the middle of the bay. San Juan de Ulúa it was called, with its massive walls deeply submerged in the bay itself. It constituted the most abominable prison in Christendom, worse by far than the Bastille in Paris or Newgate in London. Indeed, it competed with those even more dreadful dungeons in Constantinople or the hell-holes of Samarkand.

So many of Mexico's leaders would spend their formative years in San Juan de Ulúa that one of the most frequent passages in Mexican biography was: 'After two years in San Juan de Ulúa he became president,' or 'general of the armies,' or 'governor of the treasury.' This prison was the university where Mexican leaders took their advanced degrees.

If the climate of Veracruz had been salubrious, the city would have been one of the adornments of the New World, the equal of Rio de Janeiro, but the health situation was so deplorable that even the most stalwart Mexican could face a life expectancy of less than thirty years if he persisted in living there. Even lesser businessmen like López the mortgage broker had to have a second home in the hills to which they could repair during the summer. His was in Xalapa, and there were few small towns in Mexico with more charm.

It lay about sixty miles inland from Veracruz, on the extreme eastern edge of the *altoplano*, an elevation which eliminated the health problems of the seaport. The doorway leading into the central courtyard of the López home faced south to the glorious snow-covered Pico de Orizaba, 18,858 feet high, a perfect cone-shaped volcano, rising above the jungle.

Xalapa had decorative parks, winding lanes, and unexpected fountains. At dusk people sang in the squares and there was an air of liberation from the terrible heat of Veracruz. It was a somnolent town, and the birthplace of the broker's son, Antonio López de Santa-Anna Pérez de Lebrón, whose names certainly masked his reputed Spanish Gypsy ancestry.

Mexico in these turbulent years was a fascinating mix of four distinct groups. Atop the heap, and by a precipitous distance, stood the *peninsular*, born in Spain of some distinguished family of pure Spanish blood—no Moors or Jews in the background—and resident in Mexico for only a limited period while he held a senior position in the church, the army or the government. Nicknamed a *gachupín* from his habit of wearing spurs reminiscent of the spurs on the legs of fighting cocks, he ran Mexico, stole as many public funds as he could, then scurried back to Spain to enrich his family.

Lower in the hierarchy came the *criollos*, or Creoles, those of unsullied Spanish blood but born, regretfully, in Mexico. They could be educated, clever, wonderful contributors to the general weal, but they could never reach a top position because they were not *peninsulares*. Santa Anna and his family were *criollos*.

Next, and much larger in number than the top two groups, came the *mestizos*, the half-castes or mixed ones. In these years they were beginning to aspire to power but had not yet quite achieved it, although later the more gifted

42

were to attain positions of considerable importance, even the presidency.

At the bottom of the pecking order came the Indians, called *indios*. They were often quite primitive people, lacking shoes, alphabets, and leadership. But they were on the move, on the rise, and in the middle years of the century one of their number, the great Benito Juárez, a full-blooded Indian, would set Mexico on its predestined course as a nation of majestic mixed bloods.

As a *criollo*, halfway up the ladder of respectability, neither proud *peninsular* nor lowly *mestizo*, Santa Anna would spend his early years fighting for position. He did not spend much time in Mexico's inadequate schools and in later years boasted he had educated himself. He also claimed he had read only one book: adoring biographers claimed it was Caesar's *Gallic Wars*. Certainly Santa Anna had little formal education, but in its place he acquired both an uncanny ability to sense what was going to happen next and an ability to judge what his most advantageous reaction should be. When his businesslike father procured a position for him with a Veracruz merchant, he was able to sense even at the early age of fourteen that such employment was disadvantageous to his career. Santa Anna quit on the reasonable grounds that 'I was not born to be a counter-jumper.'

At a very early age—he claimed fourteen,

records suggest sixteen—he enlisted in the contingent of Royal Spain's overseas army stationed in Mexico and relished the prospect of a long life of service to the king. Because he was of Spanish blood and from a family known to be gentry, he was invited into the officers' corps, where he served in the lowest rank with distinction. In later life he described two governing principles of his life: 'I have, since my earliest years, been drawn to the glorious career of arms, feeling it to be my true vocation.' And somewhat more histrionically: 'A noble sentiment, lacking all personal ambition, constantly directed all my actions: the love of liberty and the desire to glorify the name of my country.'

During this early period in his career, Santa Anna was by personal conviction a defender of Spain, a royalist, a believer in strong central government, a devout Catholic, and one who inherently distrusted the common people, especially those of mixed or Indian blood.

He was highly pleased, therefore, when in 1811 he received orders to Veracruz as a subaltern for an expedition being assembled by Colonel Joaquín Arredondo to subjugate insurrections launched in the northern provinces by republican rebels. Such an expedition against his own people induced in Santa Anna no confusion of purpose. He said: 'The rabble have threatened to take arms against the king and must be disciplined.'

For two years he campaigned in the north

44

with Arredondo's army, chastising rebels, shooting as many of the enemy as possible and rounding up the rest, executing them or sending them off whimpering to the mines. The task was made easier when the rebels had few guns, ammunition or horses, for then the king's cavalry was free to run wild with its flashing sabers.

Santa Anna, unfortunately, was in the infantry, a despicable position for a young hopeful with Spanish blood, but he behaved with such exemplary courage that early in 1812 he was recommended for a battlefield commission to second lieutenant and, on 7 October of that same year, promoted to first lieutenant. Next he was promoted on merit to the cavalry where his imaginative command of terrain and battle tactics led to many victories, one in late 1812 when he found himself leading only thirty fellow cavalrymen into a narrow gorge in which three hundred Indians were well-entrenched. Dismissing the option of retreat, Santa Anna led a wild charge, rampaging through the gorge stabbing and slashing until his troop had chopped up and routed the Indians.

On another occasion it was *peninsular* General Arredondo who established the pattern when he found himself faced by a disorderly mass of republican revolutionaries who had dared to convene in an attempt to gain some of the freedoms voiced by Father Hidalgo, the little priest who in 1810 had issued his famous

47

Grito de Dolores, the shout from the town of Dolores, which launched Mexico's fight for independence from Spain. (He was executed for his efforts, but his movement resulted in Mexico's freedom in 1821.) When the rebels were surrounded by Arredondo's cavalry, about half were killed outright, half the remainder were shot as prisoners, and the rest were sentenced to a life of servitude in the mines. On yet another occasion, Santa Anna and the other officers rounded up an entire village from which rebels had issued forth. After shooting most of the inhabitants, regardless of their participation, Arredondo, in the military fashion of that day, ordered the survivors sent to slavery in the building of a fortress.

For almost three years Santa Anna campaigned across northern Mexico, bringing extermination instead of justice, delivering the lash, the saber, and the bullet in place of the needed reconciliation. In late July 1813, this battle-hardened unit received word that potentially dangerous efforts at rebellion had been launched beyond the Rio Grande in the province of Tejas, and with what amounted to joy Arredondo and his men headed north, with young Santa Anna once again bent on the destruction of Indians and the subjugation of any rebels who dared question the authority of the Spanish army.

Chapter 3

The Raven Preens
Its Feathers

 IN 1812, WHEN HOUSTON WAS NINE-teen, he astonished rural Tennessee with an act that demonstrated the insolence with which he treated society: To pay off his debts he opened a school. Never himself having completed a full year of education, he nevertheless presumed to teach others on the grounds that he could figure, knew the English language better than most, and could recite large portions of the *Iliad*. When he set the fees for his school, parents learned they were two dollars higher than any other in the district, eight dollars a term to be paid in three portions: cash, corn at thirty-three and one third cents a bushel, and cloth of varied colors for the teacher's clothing.

It seemed highly unlikely that such a bold

49

venture could prosper, but the would-be teacher was so tall, so stern of voice, and so capable at keeping order among unruly children that his roster was quickly filled and the school enjoyed an obvious success. With a sourwood cudgel in his hand, dressed in rough trousers and a long hunting jacket, hair braided in a long queue down his back, he dared his scholars not to learn. He said later that this was one of the happiest periods of his life, but he must have worked at night to keep one day ahead of his students.

A traditional scholar he was not. When he tried to grapple with geometry, he found its theoretical reasoning too difficult and could not get past the first abstract problem. Even so, at the end of the first year it was obvious that this Homer-spouting backwoodsman would be able to continue his school with considerable profit but, like young Santa Anna down in Veracruz, he longed for the excitement of battle. The United States was again at war with England, and reports of the eastern engagements filtered into the west. When he heard that fellow Tennessean General Andrew Jackson was fighting both the British and the Indians, Houston closed his school and lifted from the drumhead of the recruiting sergeant the silver dollar that obligated him to obey military law from then on.

By associating himself with Andrew Jackson he acquired a model for his military and political behavior. Jackson had been a lawyer, a judge, a general, a deadly duelist, an avid horse racer, a heavy drinker, and a frontier political haranguer. Adopting Jackson's style, Houston would master most of those skills.

He entered the United States army in its lowest rank, but in less than four weeks his imposing size and knowledge of guns brought him promotion to drill sergeant. He soon became an officer, and as an ensign in his first battle followed his major in a mad dash against enemy ramparts. The major was shot dead at point-blank range, but Houston carried on and won the position. In doing so he took a heavily barbed Indian arrow in his left thigh, half an inch from the groin.

'Pull it out!' he shouted at a lieutenant nearby, but this hesitant officer, after giving only two tugs, cried: 'Impossible. It'll have to be cut out.'

'Pull, damn it!' yelled Houston, reaching for his sword to force the nervous superior officer to do the job. Placing one foot against Houston's leg, the officer grabbed the arrow with both hands and jerked with all his strength. Out it came, bringing with it so much torn flesh that Houston almost fainted. A surgeon, packing the gaping hole with cotton, commanded him to 'Lie here till the battle's over.' General Jackson passing by in hurried inspection of his troops before the final push, took one look at Houston's wound and also ordered him to stay out of the battle.

But Houston could not remain inactive while

a fight was raging. Struggling to his feet, his wound dripping blood, he rushed haphazardly into the fray and found himself leading a forlorn charge up a ravine, at the far end of which the enemy waited, well ensconced. In trying to force the position, Houston took a full volley which shattered his right arm and sent a large bullet into his right shoulder.

Because of his conspicuous bravery at this crucial Battle of Horseshoe Bend in 1814, he was promoted both to lieutenant and to the close friendship of General Jackson, whose rising star he would follow thereafter. As a young officer familiar with Indian ways, he was dispatched as government spokesman to his old friends, the Indians of the Cherokee Nation, to explain the new treaties the United States was offering them. Gladly he resumed the breech-clout-and-blanket way of life, and in this mood and costume he reported to Washington in 1818 as an interpreter to help conclude arrangements profitable to both Indians and the American army.

Wearing Indian dress, his hair in a long Cherokee queue adorned with shells, he presented his chieftains to President Monroe. Although the president was pleased with Houston's effectiveness, the secretary of war was outraged and at the close of the meeting asked Houston to remain.

The secretary was John C. Calhoun, the brilliant, acidulous, furiously ambitious politician from South Carolina, one of the ablest men ever to aspire to the presidency only to lose it because of his venomous personality and his shift from a broad nationalism to a narrow, southern, pro-slavery stance. 'How dare an officer of the United States army appear in his nation's capital in such garb?'

'I came with Indians, representing Indians. They trust me because I too am an Indian.'

'Never appear before me again in such obscene dress.'

'Sir, I was able to conclude this treaty . . .'

'I am your commanding officer,' the tight-lipped, beady-eyed secretary snapped, 'and I command you to get out of that debasing costume.'

Instead, Houston got out of the army, for he would accept such speech from no one, not even General Jackson, and certainly not from some scrawny, arrogant politician. Still dressed in Indian robes, he soon penned his letter of resignation to Calhoun, initiating an enmity that would color American politics for two generations. Sam Houston hated John C. Calhoun and worked to deny him the presidency; Calhoun despised Houston and reveled in the disasters that were to overtake him.

Houston's resignation took effect in 1818, when he was twenty-five with no land, no job, no wife, and very few prospects. Within a few weeks, however, he had persuaded a Nashville lawyer of considerable reputation, Judge James Trimble, to instruct him in law. The judge spelled out the eighteen-month course of study required in those days and Sam plunged in, read assiduously, and at the end of six months announced he had learned all there was to learn and that he was prepared to serve the people of Tennessee as a lawyer. After a cursory examination of the young giant, Judge Trimble and his associates at the Nashville bar agreed.

One of the first things he did as a lawyer was to write several hell-blistering letters to Secretary of War Calhoun, demanding to know why moneys owed him by the War Department had not been paid. One letter ended: 'I can see no reason for the conduct pursued by you. . . . I could have forgotten the unprovoked injuries inflicted upon me if you were not disposed to continue them. . . . Your personal bad treatment, your official injustice I will remember as a man.'

One startling aspect of Houston's years as a young lawyer was rarely referred to but, in view of his later deportment, was of marked significance. When Sam was a handsome twenty-five, unmarried, well on his way to a secure profession, a group of similar young fellows launched the Dramatic Club of Nashville, whose members offered the city a variety of first-rate English and American plays. In one highly successful venture Houston was supposed to appear as a drunken, aggressive, hilarious porter in a role that had been much enlarged to allow him scope for his gift for comedy and imitation. As the time for presentation approached, he grew apprehensive about appearing before the public in a ridiculous posture, and he might have withdrawn from fear of being laughed at had not the other actors convinced him that he would prove the hit of the show because of his size, his gift with words, and his impressive voice.

He was the star, applauded by the audience, lauded by the newspapers and praised by the club's director who said publicly that he 'had never met a man who had a keener sense of the ridiculous . . . nor one who could more readily assume the ludicrous or the sublime.'

However, the Nashville play that created the deepest impression on Houston, helping form his attitudes toward honor, self-deportment, and public oratory, was the sensational success that had swept the nations of Europe as well as the cities of America. It was John Home's *Douglas*, a histrionic masterpiece of the Scottish Highlands in which various actors were accorded opportunities to move front and center to deliver orations that competed in popularity with Hamlet's 'To be or not to be.' In *Douglas*, the honest young hero, handsomely kilted, stepped forward to deliver words familiar to audiences of the time:

> My name is Norval; on the Grampian hills
> My father feeds his flock; a frugal swain
> Whose constant cares were to increase his
>   store,
> And keep his only son, myself, at home. . .

But brash young Norval would have none of this. Breaking away and plunging into battle, he uttered the cry which resounded through the theaters of the time wherever English was spoken:

Like Douglas conquer, or like Douglas die!

Houston did not play Norval; he had a lesser role as Glenvalon, but each night he heard this stirring line, this avowal of honor, and its rhythm became part of his arsenal. When he finished with the Dramatic Club of Nashville, his knowledge of oratory and his commanding presence aided his election by his fellow officers of the Tennessee Militia as their major-general. He would henceforth be General Houston, a title reinforced through bravery in the field and leadership in the barracks.

The civilian population regarded him so highly as an advocate in court that they elected him in 1823 to the United States House of Representatives from Tennessee's Ninth District. Nashville's most eligible bachelor made his maiden speech in the United States Congress in his very early thirties. What was the subject? Not some parochial Tennessee problem but the right of Greeks to seek independence from Turkish rule. Throughout his political career he would continue to advocate freedom for all . . . except black slaves.

It was felt by many and voiced publicly by some that Sam Houston's star could rise to the very zenith: senator, governor, member of a cabinet, even presidency. But in the fall of 1824 his spectacular rise foundered; his choice for the presidency, Andrew Jackson, was denied that high office by the strategy of dour John Quincy Adams of Massachusetts, a lifelong enemy of all that Houston aspired to, and Henry Clay, who wished to become secretary of state. And who became vice-president, with extraordinary powers in the inner circle? John C. Calhoun, more determined than ever to oppose the brash young congressman from Tennessee.

Undaunted, Houston plunged back into national politics with but two objectives: to make his hero Jackson president in 1828, and to make himself governor of Tennessee as soon as possible. He would also give careful consideration to finding himself a wife of whom his Tennessee constituents would approve.

Chapter 4

The Eagle Bloods Its Claws

 IF SAM HOUSTON WAS UNDERGOING A series of crucial experiences in these years, his future adversary Santa Anna was having similar experiences in Mexico. No single event in Tennessee would exert the overpowering influence on Houston that an affair in the northern province of Tejas was about to have on Santa Anna.

In August of 1813, when Santa Anna was nineteen, his brutal and vengeful leader Arredondo crossed the Rio Grande at Laredo and marched north to punish republican rebels at San Antonio de Béxar. As General Arredondo penetrated those furnace-hot dusty plains, his resolve hardened. Summoning his officers one evening when the little capital still lay three days distant he harangued them:

Who are these rebels? Let's face facts. There are nearly thirty-two hundred of them, only two thousand of us. But do not lose heart, for we are trained military men, with many battles behind us, with strict discipline, with knowledge of operations, and with Gómez Padilla here with his six cannon. The advantage is all with us.

So I ask again, who are these rebels? Seventeen hundred are Mexican citizens of Spanish blood who've gained the idea that they can establish some kind of free state up here, excused from the laws we issue in Mexico City. They must be crushed, and I want no prisoners.

Six hundred of the others are deluded Indians who are always ready to fight for any big word . . . like freedom . . . or liberty . . . words they couldn't define if you asked them. Kill what you have to, the rest will run away, so let them go. We don't want them cluttering up our lines.

The other nine hundred? Now here's the ugly problem. I'm told they're mostly Americans who have sneaked in over the border at Louisiana . . . many of them cutthroats, bandits, thieves, renegades. If their own government caught them they'd all be hanged for crimes committed there. Now they try to steal Tejas and they must be chastised. No prisoners. When this battle is over I want a solemn gasp to spread from Louisiana to Washington. 'So this is what happens when outsiders invade Mexico.' I want the Americans to know what they're up against if they dare to touch our sacred soil.

When he finished this tirade, his face red with passion, he more calmly issued a series of crisp directives to his officers which revealed both his plan for an annihilating battle and his considerable competency as a field leader:

We shall approach the rebels with only a few of our troops visible in the front ranks. Lieutenants Moncado and Santa Anna will be in command, and when the fighting grows intense, they will retreat, as if overwhelmed.

We can be sure the rabble will accept our bait. They will come crashing after our retreating men, and at that moment I rush forward with our entire force and crush the rebels. Then ... annihilation, with the six cannon of Gómez Padilla smashing them to bits.

Lieutenant Moncado recognized the brilliance of this proposal were it to be executed against a true rabble who could be expected to chase any fleeing figure, but he had read two books about the sophistication with which American armies had battled the English in the war of 1776. He warned General Arredondo that if this republican army at San Antonio, so superior in numbers, had American leadership comparable to that in their war against the English, the trap might not work and it could be the exposed Spanish troops who would be annihilated.

Ah, my son! You're right! If the Americans and their deluded Mexican allies had real leadership. . . . But tell me, who were the leaders of the Americans in the 1776 war you speak of? Frenchmen and Germans and Poles. They taught the stupid Americans how to fight. That mob up there has no Lafayette, and this time they'll be facing a Spanish army.

By the accidents of the battle, with neither side making a conscious choice of site or relative advantage, the two armies stumbled together on a broad field near the little Río Medina. The rabble, sensing that they well outnumbered the government forces, launched an assault on Arredondo's formation. Because of their fine marksmanship, the Kentucky and

Tennessee vagrants succeeded in driving back Lieutenant Moncado on the Spanish left and Lieutenant Santa Anna on the right. In fact, the Spanish army was so heavily hit that its ranks broke and a general retreat began.

'After them, men!' an American voice shouted from amidst the rebel front.

'¡Ataque!' cried a Spanish officer, leaping forward.

Then came the harsh, commanding voice of another, saner American: 'Men! For Christ's sake stop! It's a trap!' The man tried his best to halt the mad plunge forward, but accomplished nothing. He was still shouting 'Trap! Trap!' when the tail end of the American horde swept past him.

The so-called Battle of Medina was a sickening affair, for almost every one of General Arredondo's men did precisely as ordered: Santa Anna and Moncado closed the trap; Gómez Padilla fired his cannon right into the heart of the confused rebellion, and Arredondo himself dispatched extra troops to any spot in the Spanish lines which seemed likely to bend or break.

Despite great carnage the Spanish army could not kill all the men within its trap, and some of the rebels broke free through sheer weight of numbers. As they fled across the fields, Arredondo unleashed his skilled cavalry, which ran down the Americans and the Mexicans as if they were rabbits or wild pigs. The Indians they ignored, for they could be counted upon to fade harmlessly back into the endless plains, if they survived.

The tremendous victory that August day would of itself have made a profound impression on young Santa Anna, for it proved what a disciplined army trained in European tactics could achieve against a collection of American adventurers and misguided provincials calling for equality with the *peninsulares*, but it was the following slaughters that made the indelible imprint.

When the cavalry rounded up several hundred fleeing rebels, including many Americans, the grizzled leader of the Spanish horsemen ordered the prisoners to dig a long, shallow ditch across which timbers were stretched. Onto these timbers scores of prisoners were marched and then gunned down by firing squads who performed so efficiently that the corpses pitched headfirst into the waiting ditch.

That night Arredondo crammed more than three hundred other prisoners into an improvised jail within the town of San Antonio. By morning eighteen had suffocated or been strangled by the pressure of other bodies. About half the survivors were dragged into the public square and shot; the others were put to work on the roads.

American soldiers were executed wherever caught, but the thing that most impressed Santa Anna was General Arredondo's harsh treatment of any civilians who were suspected

of having supported the rebels to even the slightest degree—they were summarily shot. When the multiple executions ended, the general indicated that his troops could enjoy the town, which they did by looting, by raping in the public streets, and by the inventive punishment of gathering together in a kind of jail all the older gentlewomen of the town, who were forced for eighteen days to do laundry for the victors and bake them tortillas* while the soldiers laughed.

Santa Anna, watching the completeness of this victory—the masterful manner in which the Americans were defeated, the ineffectiveness of the Mexican proletariat, and the harshness with which the civilian population was punished whether guilty or not—gained the idea that this was the effective way to handle even mild protests. But perhaps the most significant of his reactions was the contempt he generated for Americans in general.

The unquestioned honors that Santa Anna won at Medina were somewhat sullied by the fact that, while he was still in San Antonio enjoying the victory and pillage, General Arredondo discovered that the young officer who was becoming his favorite lieutenant had fal-

---

*A distinguished woman scholar has recently said: 'I always suspect that "making tortillas" for the victors was a 19th century euphemism for rape.'

sified the books of his regiment in order to cover gambling debts. Santa Anna had for some time escaped detection by forging Arredondo's signature to a check to cover the deficiency, saying to himself: 'The general will be too busy to look into a thing like this.'

Santa Anna would have been dismissed from the army had not a military surgeon advanced him the money to cover the check; Santa Anna later repaid him in part but never in full.

However, matters of much greater importance now impinged, for Mexican patriots were beginning to assemble the power to throw off the Spanish yoke, not because they hated the mother country's government, one of the most congenial among the empires controlled by European nations, but because Spain insisted upon sending to high positions in Mexico officials who were abominably incompetent. The native-born *criollos* and *mestizos* were no longer satisfied with being denied the top positions in government, church, and army. As one young *criollo* aspirant said: 'It isn't that we despise the incompetent *peninsulares* sent out from Spain. We also hate the competent ones. They must stay in Spain and let us run the country.'

So in the years 1813–1821 Mexico found itself immersed in a slow, seething turmoil not quite revolution but certainly not peace. Santa Anna's position in these semi-turbulent times consisted of three tenets which he was ready to defend. In a cynical self-serving man-

ner he defended the Spanish monarchy, aware
that, for the present at least, it represented
the source of power. However, on the field of
battle he demonstrated repeatedly that his al-
legiance to Spain was not stinting. He was
prepared to lay down his life for the king, and
very nearly did on several heroic occasions.

He defended the Catholic church in much
the same way. A prudent rather than a devout
believer, he respected the church as a source
of power in public life and a treasury upon
which he could draw in time of trouble. He
could not comprehend why other nations were
Protestant.

Despite growing convictions in Mexico that
the *fueros*, the special privileges for the clergy
and military, should be ended, he continued to
believe that the welfare of Mexico depended
upon continuance of special courts in which
priests and army officers were tried with little
chance of being found guilty; in simplest terms,
clerics and military were above the civil law.
These were the basic concepts on which he
had been reared and he swore never to abandon them.

He did diverge from Spanish leadership on
one trivial point: he thought it might be helpful if responsibility for Mexico's government
were placed in the hands of persons born
in Mexico—not *mestizos* or *indios*, God for-
bid—but men of pure-blooded Spanish inheri-
tance like himself. The battle cry he uttered
sometimes in the barracks was: *'¡Abajan los*

Gachupines! Arriba la Religión y los Fueros!'
(Down with the peninsulars from Spain! Up
with the Catholic church and the rights protected by the special courts!)

By 1820 the Spanish-speaking world was in
a state of chaos. In the homeland, progressive
elements forced a repressive king to yield freedoms. The men of an army unit already on the
dock in Spain, with orders to board ship to
fight revolutionary uprisings in the American
colonies, refused to sail and their officers supported them, refusing also to enter the ship.

Colonies long loyal to Spain now broke away
to establish new nations throughout South
America, still Spanish but free to follow new
patterns. In Mexico these new movements
produced a confusion into which Santa Anna
was soon drawn. *Peninsulares* newly arrived
from Spain and contaminated by liberal ideas
sweeping the homeland, generated new ani-
mosities among local conservatives when they
endeavored to introduce into Mexico the reforms which had become common in Spain.
Specifically, when these *peninsulares* wanted
to terminate a carryover from the old days—
no more special privileges for the church or
the military—conservative groups throughout
Mexico felt obligated to resist.

As a result, while homeland Spain became
more liberal, colonial Mexico drew back in
reaction until everyone except extreme right-
ists like Santa Anna began to realize that the
nation could no longer be governed from Ma-

drid. Men listened when a wonderfully handsome, charismatic Mexican-born officer named Agustín de Iturbide, a general of course, issued his famous *Plan de Iguala* calling for separation from Spain and for sensible reforms under a ruler who lived in Mexico. Although soldiers from all quarters flocked to Iturbide, Santa Anna remained steadfast in his support of the monarchy . . . for one month.

At the beautiful little mountain town of Orizaba, at the foot of the volcano of that name and not far from Xalapa, Santa Anna gave proof of his royalist loyalty, for at four o'clock one morning he personally led a sortie which surprised and humiliated the Mexican rebels, for which gallantry the Spanish promoted him to lieutenant-colonel.

He spent the rest of that cool morning reflecting on affairs in Mexico and on the fact that the rebels had not fled as expected but had reinforced their army for a return assault which could come at any time. He continued to study the situation during a hasty lunch, and by two that afternoon his mind was clear and resolute. He marched his men out of Orizaba and joined the rebels, for which act of good judgment they promoted him to full colonel. Thus within twelve explosive hours Santa Anna jumped two grades, from major to colonel, in two different armies defending two radically different principles.

By such events did Spain's rule die in Mexico. For three centuries, 1519–1821, Spain had

sent to the New World great leaders like Cortés and Coronado, stout administrators like Mendoza, sanctified friars and priests and hundreds of loyal, hopeful laymen. Its contribution had been enormous—roads, presidios in the desert, a great university in the capital, suppression of banditry, glorious buildings glistening white in the sun, a religion that bound all parts together, one of the most melodious and loving languages in the world, order—and now its golden sun had set. But its influence on Mexico would be everlasting, and the impression it left on one of its most distant provinces, Tejas, would be permanent too. Much of the charm of later Texas, its style of dress, its food, its locutions, its manner of ranching practices, would stem from the centuries it had been Spanish. The gold of Spain would reflect from a thousand sites and in the smiles of a million inhabitants.

When Iturbide, trained by Spain, overthrew Spanish rule in 1821, Colonel Santa Anna became vociferous in his support, echoing Iturbide's cries for freedom, for the Church, and for equality among all Mexicans. When he first came into Iturbide's presence his soldiers heard Santa Anna shout:

> Beloved Iturbide, whom all Mexico loves, we place ourselves, our guns and our lives at your disposal, for only you can give Mexico the strong and just rule it yearns for. The blood will run

drop by drop from my body in defense of your noble and heroic effort. Long live Iturbide! Long live freedom! Long live the glories of a new day!

When Iturbide decided to crown himself Emperor of Mexico after a brief spell as a kind of military dictator, Santa Anna was one of the first to realize that what he had always really wanted was a native-born emperor. He not only led the cheering for the slim, handsome fellow of limited intelligence who mounted the throne, but also submitted this written testimonial:

Immortal Iturbide! All Mexico rejoices at the step you have taken. You bring us light and hope. It is true that there may be a few discordant elements who lack true patriotism and any knowledge of the duties of citizens but I and my army stand ready to help you eliminate them.

Your Majesty must be aware that I am and will be throughout my life your loyal defender who will embrace death in your defense. Your loyal subject who throws himself at the illustrious feet of Your Majesty.

Ant. López de Santa Anna
General of the Armies

His rise to general had been spectacular and merited. At his beloved city of Veracruz he repelled an attempt by a contingent of the Spanish army, still held up in the fortress of San Juan de Ulúa, to regain the city, and from this engagement he emerged a national hero of serious dimensions. As such it was advisable that he take a wife, for he was now twenty-eight and still unmarried, a condition not viewed favorably in Spanish countries. With the innate ability he had for manipulation, he now laid furious, poetic, and romantic court to Emperor Iturbide's spinster sister, Doña Nicolasa, sixty years old, thin, ugly, and suddenly rich. His ardent courtship became the talk of Mexico until the lady dismissed the flower-bearing general one morning with the curt comment: 'Don't be silly.' The Emperor said the same.

In that same period, Iturbide gave Santa Anna a more serious rebuff, for when the heroic young general, covered with medals, came before him for an audience, Santa Anna thoughtlessly sat down, whereupon a member of the imperial court reprimanded him: 'Señor Brigadier, no one sits in the presence of an Emperor.'

From such small beginnings a deep rift developed between ultra-loyal Santa Anna and his beloved Emperor. Before the first year of the monarchy was out, Santa Anna was again conspiring, swaying toward agreement with the growing popular demand for a new form of government, this time a republic. With the prevailing winds blowing toward federalism, Santa Anna now bent to the realization that Mexico's real destiny lay not with a local emperor such as European nations had, but with a republic like that of the United States.

In this political and moral confusion Santa Anna felt constrained to turn against his benefactor, and he watched sadly as Iturbide was banished forever from Mexico with a generous pension to be paid in Italy. But when the self-deceived dandy tried to slip back into the country and recover his throne, Santa Anna did not object when he was shot. Witnesses reported that shortly before the execution Santa Anna had been heard to mutter: 'We shall soon see if no one sits down in the presence of an Emperor.' Mexicans were beginning to learn that when Santa Anna promised to defend a colleague to the death, it was the colleague's death about which he spoke.

It is a matter of supreme importance in the life of Santa Anna that in 1824 he vigorously supported a new republican constitution which would henceforth govern Mexico. It was a document formed in the American pattern, and noteworthy in that it called for a substantial degree of sovereignty for the individual states, one of which was to be the newly formed state of Coahuila-y-Tejas with its first capital in the lovely city of Saltillo. Santa Anna became a strong defender of this decentralization and predicted bright futures for the states, which were at last to be free from complete central domination.

In this new climate he presented himself as a man who had undergone a moral and intellectual awakening. He acted as if he now understood when liberals cried that the Catholic church had to be divested of its vast land holdings and why separate courts for priests and soldiers could no longer be tolerated. He also nodded when reformers argued: 'Indians must have equal rights.' In short, he posed as a powerful voice for democracy, justice, and responsible rule throughout Mexico.

His leaps from Spanish royalist to Mexican imperialist to basic republican had been gargantuan, but they had been accompanied by two invariables: He was indubitably brave, facing bullets when necessary; and whenever he joined a new side he offered its leaders his life's blood in their defense, as he did now: 'In support of our new republican freedoms and the justices which accompany them, I shall forever stand ready to surrender my life itself.'

It was ominous, however, when he confided to an associate: 'I have no idea what a republic is. A lawyer in Xalapa told me it was a good thing.'

Chapter 5

The Raven Topples

 WHILE GENERAL SANTA ANNA WAS leaping up the ladder in Mexico, General Houston was doing at least as well in Tennessee. Reelected to Congress in 1825, and promoted to the governorship of Tennessee in 1827, he played a significant role in preparing the way for the election of his friend Andrew Jackson to the presidency in 1828. Tall, of commanding presence, talented in debate, and reliable as a friend, he could foresee no hindrance to his enormous ambition, and his associates were already speaking of him as a likely candidate for the presidency if Jackson, widely believed to be too infirm to hold office for long, did not win a second term. This was not an idle dream, for Tennessee played a vital role in national politics. Representing the growing power of the new west, it would send three sons to the presidency: Andrew Jackson, James K. Polk, and Andrew Johnson. Sam Houston could well have been added to that list. In a state of limited political leverage like New Jersey he would have had little chance; in Tennessee he had all before him.

He was curiously like Santa Anna in his reluctance to marry. He was now in his thirty-fifth year and still a bachelor, and he heard friends whisper that it was imprudent for a man to hold the exalted position of governor without a wife to aid him. After many false starts and tentative engagements, therefore, he settled upon a most winsome young woman from a leading family in Gallatin, a few miles northeast of Nashville. Eliza Allen was exactly half Houston's age, a modest, attractive girl with a good education, a sensitive spirit, and a longing to be married. Unfortunately, it was not Houston she wished to wed; her heart had been given to a poetic young man of immense charm, genteel bearing, and the romantic allure of a lingering illness that would kill him within a few years.

But the Allen family, a large one, was so enchanted by the prospect of a daughter's marrying a governor that they exerted on Eliza more pressure than was proper. With hidden tears and the most profound remorse she made her parents happy by accepting Houston. When the tall, handsome governor stood beside the delicate little Eliza to face the minister, all doubts as to the propriety of such a marriage were dissolved. Indeed, so elated was Houston that eight days later he announced his determination to stand for re-election, and so popular did the marriage make him throughout the state that his election to a second term as governor, and later to the United States Senate, seemed assured.

The Houstons were married in January 1829; on 16 April of that year, during the heat of the election campaign, Eliza startled Tennessee, and the rest of the United States too, by abruptly terminating their marriage and fleeing in tears to her father's house in Gallatin. That day Sam Houston resigned the governorship and withdrew from the race for a second term.

He gave no explanation, then or ever. Some cyclonic difference had come between husband and wife, and he refused on a point of honor to state what it was; she likewise kept silent. He was besieged by friends who assured him if only he would speak they could clear the atmosphere and reinstate him in the election with a guarantee of victory: 'Look at what Andy Jackson did. The scandal of his marriage was certainly worse than yours, and he survived, although he had to kill a man to do so.'

Houston had almost killed his man, too, for he prized honor above all, and in those years

such men found it difficult to avoid duels. Some years before, a shadowy political hack had crossed his trail in Nashville, said something improper and then hired a professional duelist from Missouri to deliver a challenge to Houston, who appointed his own second, a stuffy colonel with a meticulous understanding of the honor code. Harrumphing up to the imported Missouri gunman, he said, correctly: 'General Houston can receive no challenge from your hands because you are not a citizen of this state.'

By a series of tricks the Missourian then enlisted the services of a distinguished general with an honorable record, one William A. White, and it was this man, third in line, who finally issued the challenge, even though he himself had no quarrel with Houston and was in no way involved with the shady politician. Why did Houston go ahead with such a ridiculous duel? His explanation reveals much about the moral climate of the time: 'Knowing that a coward cannot live except in disgrace and obscurity I did not hesitate as to my course.' On the flimsiest point of honor White continued to demand a duel and was shocked when Houston, with the right to choose weapons and distances, elected pistols at a murderous fifteen feet. At that distance a marksman could hardly miss anyone as huge as Houston, but friends whispered: 'Good old Sam. Always thinking. By choosing among his three challengers he winds up with the poorest shot of the lot.'

It was a real duel. General White, almost fainting with fear, fired and missed. General Houston fired and plugged his man in the groin. 'You have killed me,' White whimpered. 'I am very sorry,' Houston said, looking down at him, 'but you know it was forced upon me.' The fallen general said: 'I know it, and forgive you.' He did not die.

Houston's indictment by a grand jury in Kentucky on the spurious grounds that the duel had occurred in that jurisdiction was an act of political vengeance by Henry Clay's people, who hated Houston for his work in defense of Andrew Jackson. Nothing came of the indictment, but the duel and its complicated surroundings demonstrated the peculiar code of honor that operated at this time.

Now Eliza's brother and uncle volunteered to duel Houston in defense of their sister's honor, a catastrophe that he avoided by assuring them that no dishonor attached to their sister, only to him. Then he challenged the entire state of Tennessee: 'I will fight anybody, anywhere who dares to speak a word against my wife.'

But his challenge did not lay to rest the nagging question of honor. The good citizens of Gallatin, offended that any cloud should hang over one of their loveliest daughters, did something that astonished Tennessee. They assembled a formal, public committee charged with the following grave responsibility:

> Resolved, that the following gentlemen be appointed a committee to consider and draw up a report expressive of the opinion entertained of the private virtues of Mrs. Eliza A. Houston and whether her amiable character had received an injury among those acquainted with her, in consequence of the late unfortunate occurrence between her and her husband, General Samuel Houston, late Governor of Tennessee.

The twelve-man committee, which took its duties most gravely, consisted of two generals, two colonels, a major, a captain, five distinguished lawyers, and one private citizen.

The committee met over a period of forty-eight hours, listened to witnesses, assessed the situation as best they could on partial evidence, and concluded that Eliza Allen Houston of Gallatin, Tennessee, was a virtuous woman, that she had behaved with decorum, that no aspersions could be cast against her honor, and that she must be considered by society as merely one more injured female. By a vote of twelve to nil they certified that she was unsullied.

The committee also recommended that a

copy of their formal, many-paragraphed decision be broadcast to all newspapers that had taken an interest in the affair, but they prudently refrained from mailing their report until Houston was safely out of the state.

With time, several facts have emerged about this extraordinary affair. Although neither Sam nor Eliza ever spoke publicly about the disaster, certain conclusions can be tentatively reached. The difference could not have been what many at the time thought, some grave sexual impotency; each partner later married someone else, with Eliza bearing two or perhaps three children and Sam fathering eight. There is solid ground for suspecting that Governor Houston came home unexpectedly one day to find his wife sobbing over a collection of old love letters from that frail poet-like young fellow she now realized she should have married. Houston, appalled that the governor of a great state like Tennessee should be thus humiliated, seems to have shouted at her and she to him, after which they parted.

But a Mrs. Robert Martin of their hometown had a much different story, which she told at the time, and to many citizens: 'Governor Houston was outside being peppered with snowballs thrown at him by my two daughters. As Eliza and I watched, I teased her about her husband's plight, and she told me: "I wish they would kill him." I looked up astonished to hear such a remark from a bride of only forty-eight hours, but she repeated in the same voice: "Yes, I wish from the bottom of my heart that they would kill him."'

It seems indubitable that he was the one who threw her out, for some years later she was to try valiantly to effect a reconciliation but he refused.*

He resolved the pitiful affair dramatically. Ex-governor of a focal state, ex-congressman, personal friend of the president, he took a steamer down the Tennessee River, the Ohio and the Mississippi, then up the Arkansas to resume residence among the only people who understood him, the people of the Cherokee Nation, among whom he would reside for three years of painful and reviled exile.

On 17 December 1831 the brilliant Frenchman Alexis de Tocqueville, who probably un-

---

*In 1982 during a hunting trip in Florida I shared quarters with a lineal descendant of Eliza Allen's family, who confided: 'One morning while my father was shaving he told me: "There's something you must know. We've passed it along from father to son all these years. The real reason why General Houston and our ancestor broke up was explained to our family by the doctor in the case. Houston had a very ugly suppurating sore in his right shoulder which could not be cured. Indian bullet in one of the battles with General Jackson. He was a big, rough, brutal man and Eliza was a lovely little southern belle half his age. She just couldn't take him and his dreadful ways. And he told her that if she felt that way to get out."'

derstood American democracy better than anyone then alive, was drifting down the Mississippi River when the steamboat on which he was traveling was hailed by a grubby vessel coming out of the Arkansas River. From it climbed a very tall, gaunt man, unshaven and dressed in ragged Indian garb. His hair was long, his nails dirty, his manner contemptuous. He seems to have spent time with de Tocqueville, who remembered him as the most horrible example he had seen of one of the worst aspects of democracy: 'When the right of suffrage is universal, and when the deputies are paid by the state, it is singular how low and how far wrong the people can go.' He referred to Houston, this broken ex-governor, as the personification of the unpleasant consequences of democracy.

De Tocqueville was right in his assessment of Houston during this period; the Cherokees themselves had given Houston a second name, Big Drunk, a pejorative freely bandied about in those frontier days when men were accustomed to consume what some bystanders judged 'an excessive amount.'

Among the Cherokees, Houston, the drunken exile, opened a little store, as a hundred white squaw men had done before, and lived most happily, when not drunk, with a Cherokee woman named Tiana Rogers.

He never married Tiana in any legal Christian ceremony, for he was still legally married to Eliza Allen, but he certainly married her in the Cherokee tradition and was known throughout the Nation as her husband. In any case it is highly unlikely that he would have been interested in a church wedding because of the cruel rejection he had experienced by formal religion.

Back in 1829, during the first days of his separation from his wife and the collapse of his political dreams, he had in his despair sought consolation from the clergyman who had performed the marriage ceremony only a few months before. Dr. William Hume was not surprised that the sinner Sam Houston came before him, an abject man who had never had time to join an organized church when he was leaping from one high position to another. Now, when all had crumbled, he asked Dr. Hume to baptize him, make him an acknowledged Christian, and accept him into the Episcopal church.

Reverend Hume, taking his ecclesiastical duty very seriously, realized that this might well be a case referred to in the rhyme:

> The Devil was sick
> The Devil a monk would be.
> The Devil was well
> The Devil a monk was he.

Accordingly, he sought counsel from the Presbyterian minister, Obadiah Jennings, who urged caution, pointing out that the respectable connections of the lady in Gallatin were much offended and might take it unkindly if the church at this late date offered membership to the reprobate who had caused them embarrassment. After prolonged consideration of all the niceties involved, Reverend Hume solemnly reported to the community: 'Mr. Jennings and myself, to whom General Houston applied to be baptized, declined on good grounds.' An ex-governor of a state was refused admission to the church, or its consolation in his time of tribulation, lest such action offend the powerful members of his estranged wife's family.

Even at this nadir Houston felt obligated to respect the traditions of southern honor; when a local braggart challenged him to a duel for no sensible reason at all, Sam still felt honor-bound to accept. Seconds were appointed, and in morning haze the lengths were stepped off. The two men, obviously unsteady, marched, turned, aimed, and fired. Both missed, for the very good reason that their seconds, realizing both were drunk and that their quarrel lacked any sensible basis, had loaded the pistols only with powder, no bullets.

Houston remained drunk. One passenger traveling down the Mississippi referred to him as 'a hostage to Bacchus', and another reported that he had harangued the steamer's passengers when it stopped to take on Arkansas travelers; he wanted them to march overland to God's country in Oregon. This man reported that Houston himself was intending to head for Oregon as soon as practical. He had not at this time expressed any interest in removing to the Mexican state of Coahuila-y-Tejas.

Chapter 6

The Eagle Soars

 WHILE THE RAVEN LAY WITH INJURED wings, The Eagle soared to new heights, his feathers resplendent in the sun. He had taken to wearing the most exquisite uniforms: highly figured leather boots with gold hammered into the design, sheer white trousers closely fitted and made in France of a tough, pliable cloth, an encrusted sword made in Spain and covered with gold and silver worth more than seven thousand American dollars, a flowing sash of Persian silk again woven with flecks of gold, a shirt of pure linen made in England, a handsome ruff about the neck, and over all a tunic of brilliant red adorned by many large medals including Mexico's new Order of Guadalupe as big as a

soup plate and Spain's Order of Isabella la Ca-
tólica, small but obviously more distinguished.

Because he was inordinately vain, he had
himself painted many times, and photographed after the invention of the daguerreo-
type, so that we have a chronological record of
his adult appearance over six decades. In
not one representation does he look ordinary.
Taller than most Mexicans and sharper of eye,
he had an authentic imperial bearing, slim in
his youth, statesmanlike-heavy in his older
years. His countenance was stern and commanding; as a young man his face was thin
and patrician, but the salient feature was his
head of thick black hair which retained its
striking color throughout his life. He wore it
in the attractive style of the early nineteenth
century, brushed strongly forward at the tem-
ples and below the ears, so that his face was
always framed in black. But he was more distinguished for his overall bearing, which was
majestic, than for any particular reason.

He was entitled to half a dozen grandilo-
quent titles, and insisted upon them when being presented to the public or when drafting
one of his constant *pronunciamentos* calling
upon Mexicans to adhere to their ancient vir-
tues and make the nation strong and peaceful.
The title he relished most was one given him
by several cities, *Benemérito de Tampico*, for
example, and *Benemérito de Veracruz*, which
could be read The One Who is Well Deserving
of Tampico, or of Veracruz. He referred to him-

self as *Benemérito* in his public speeches, but also as The Eagle, a fortunate cognomen tying him to the new flag of Mexico, most colorful of all the nations', with a tricolor base of green for the beloved countryside, red for the blood of the heroes, and white for the purity of the Catholic church. The center was decorated with a handsome depiction of the ancient Mayan fable explaining the settlement of the capital city: 'You shall wander until you see an eagle perched on a cactus devouring a snake.' The embroidered eagle was stalwart, the snake writhed, and the rounded nopals of the cactus provided space for showing the names of the various states. Santa Anna intimated to his friends that he was the eagle on the flag fighting the battle against the snake of corruption.

His crusade did not, however, extend to his personal life, for on the eastern outskirts of Xalapa he had assembled a country plantation of gigantic size, Manga de Clavo (Spike of Clove), where he ran cattle innumerable and kept his wife and children in grandiose style. The precise maneuvers by which he had acquired this vast estate remain obscure; expropriation, bribery and theft all played a part, but the desired result was of awesome dimension. Like generals in all nations in all ages, he assumed that he was entitled to unusual privileges; in his case they ran to hundreds of thousands of acres, millions of pesos, and a score of mistresses.

Santa Anna was happy at Manga de Clavo,

touring his holdings on horseback and in-
dulging his passion for cock fighting. He had
unquestionably the finest covey of fighting
birds in Mexico and delighted in pitting them
against upstarts in whatever part of the country he happened to be invading. But even so,
Manga de Clavo did not entirely satisfy him,
for it stood rather far out in the countryside.
He therefore exercised his considerable powers
of persuasion on the neighboring landowners
and came up with an even finer establishment
close to town, El Encero, a more refined home
worth millions of pesos.

He was happy in his married life, for he
had found a perfect wife, a tall, thin, ungainly
woman who brought him a dowry and respectability. Fortunately, she preferred stay-
ing in Xalapa rather than venturing into the
maelstrom of Mexico City politics. Her husband could find no fault with this, because it
left him free to dally with the young women of
the capital who found him irresistible; he already had five known illegitimate children cir-
culating in polite circles, with more to follow.

Since he had now maneuvered a series of un-
broken victories in battle, including a major
victory at Tampico in 1829 when he repulsed
Spanish forces sent from Cuba by Ferdinand
VII to reconquer Mexico, in public he began to
call himself the Napoleon of the West and had
himself so painted, right hand jammed into
his vest. In whatever house he occupied he assembled memorials of that other great gen-

eral. But despite his posturing, Santa Anna possessed some of the traits of an authentic military genius. He was never afraid to face real danger, although he did have a propensity for looking at all sides of an impending battle and withdrawing his troops if he felt he could not win handsomely. More important, as a congenital opportunist he showed great skill at jumping in at the last minute when someone else had done the fighting but he could claim the victory.

The prevailing winds of Mexico's political climate continued to blow, during this period, ever stronger toward federalism, and Santa Anna pragmatically continued to bend before them. In 1833 this gaudy, heroic chameleon became president of Mexico as an advocate of the three-part liberal platform whose supporters had been gaining strength since independence in 1821: a federal system composed of self-governing states; curtailment of the rampant prerogatives of the church, and the abolishment of special courts for priests and army officers. These federalist ideas were so appealing to the general population, which longed for real freedoms and order, that the state legislatures elected him enthusiastically.

Then began a mystifying quadrille. He did not like politics and abhorred the bickering attendant upon any national assembly. A soldier and by nature a confirmed authoritarian, whenever a difficult or unpopular decision had to be made he relinquished the presidency,

mounted his horse, and rode down to Manga de Clavo, where like Achilles he sulked in his tent until such time as the populace demanded he return to save them. Then he remounted, rode up the hilly trail to Puebla and on to Mexico City, where he was invariably greeted with vast parades, the firing of cannon and the hosannahs of the multitude, and was made president once again.* After one such return he was accorded a more expansive honorific, *Benemérito de la Patria* (Well-Deserving of the Entire Country).

In the eight years 1829–1837, while the United States was having only one president—Andrew Jackson, a man of rugged character who bound his nation more firmly together—Mexico suffered seventeen: seven different men chosen by due procedure, ten who held the office temporarily while the president was absent or indisposed. This playing of musical chairs with the office of the presidency was the hideous penalty paid by most of the former Spanish colonies who were allowed to grasp their freedom before developing any theory of responsible government. Subservient to priests, bedazzled by generals, and confused

---

*Technically he would be president eleven times, if his many temporary, self-imposed retirements are considered to entail a change in the presidency. He was officially elected to the presidency five times.

by the swiftness of events, Mexico and the other former Spanish colonies sought refuge in the leadership of generals who had no keener sense of national destiny than did the muddled population. There were governments, many of them, but no governing, and since this fatal disease was so endemic throughout the Spanish world, Spain herself must stand condemned as a nation which had once possessed vast territories, had ruled them relatively well, but had failed to instill in them any capacity for self-government.

The edgy Anglo-American settlers who were crowding into the state of Coahuila-y-Tejas were aware of this chaos and disturbed by it: 'If Mexico City can't govern itself, how can it govern us way up here?' Residents in other parts of Mexico were equally distressed, and it was understandable that patriots should begin to think their nation could be governed only by some firm-minded dictator of benevolent heart. They apparently felt, eleven times, that Santa Anna fit this description. Whenever the going got rough, however, their hero's solution was to abdicate and sequester himself on his estates in Xalapa, giving his people the opportunity to see how poorly they fared without him.

Four times during the critical years when confrontation with Tejas loomed—June 1833, July 1833, December 1833, January 1836—Santa Anna walked away from the presidency but always came riding back, once with a startling revelation which he tossed before the public without embarrassment. Although he confessed he had once backed, with ardor and sincerity, the principle of freedom for the people, now he saw this was folly. Realizing that the people of Mexico were not yet ready for personal liberties, he concluded that despotism was what they needed, a despotism enforceable by him with wisdom and virtue:

> I now realize that I am a conservative and I offer the nation a clear program which will save it. We must have a strong central government in which individual states enjoy few powers, and certainly not individual legislatures. The Catholic church must rule supreme. And the ancient privileges which priests and army officers once enjoyed must be restored.

Reviving the battle cry of '*Religión y Fueros*' against which he had once campaigned, he scuttled the liberal Constitution of 1824 and overnight converted Mexico into a theocratic dictatorship . . . and the citizens applauded.

That is, most of them did. In the rich silver state of Zacatecas, a hotbed of federalism where men had relished their brief taste of self-government, they refused to abandon the Constitution of 1824 and mustered a militia to defend it.

This was the kind of challenge that Santa

Anna loved, for it presented him with an opportunity to escape the bureaucratic tangles of government, mount his horse, and charge off to do battle with a more tangible enemy. His reputation had been built on such affairs, and it was now about to be enlarged to the point of absolutism.

This time he would not enjoy numerical superiority; the Zacatecans had about thirteen thousand men under arms while he commanded less than a third of that number, three thousand five hundred. The Zacatecans also outnumbered him in cannon and had good cavalry, but he had several tricks up his military coat sleeve. He intended ripping a page out of Napoleon's book and surprising the city's defenders with a surreptitious attack from the rear, which usually unnerved nonprofessionals; he also encouraged several of his officers to leave his ranks in apparent disgust, sneak into the city, and proclaim themselves defenders of the Constitution of 1824 and enemies of Santa Anna. As trained soldiers they would be welcomed and given command of troops, whom they would lead to disaster when the fighting began.

In April 1835 Santa Anna, forty-one years old and at the height of his powers, assembled his military units at Aguascalientes, south of Zacatecas, and began a slow, determined march north. He reached the rebel city on 10 May and began an immediate assault early the next day that resulted in total victory, for

110

the attack upon its rear and the defection of its newly acquired officers left the city unable to defend itself, despite its superiority in numbers.

The aftermath of the battle reveals the savagery of Santa Anna's retribution: he turned his men loose in a wild, far-reaching rampage that burned part of the city, looted all of it, and killed some two thousand five hundred women and male non-participants. One foreign official reported: 'Our families became special targets, with English and American husbands slain and their women stripped naked and run through the streets. Rape and pillage continued for two days, until our once-fair city was a burning, screaming shambles.'

Zacatecas was punished for not having changed its mind as swiftly as General Santa Anna had changed his, and so the word went out: 'The same will happen to Tejas if it continues to clamor for the Constitution of 1824.'

When reports of the massacre at Zacatecas filtered north to the Americans who had wandered into Tejas, thoughtful citizens whispered: 'What might happen if Santa Anna marched up here to discipline us?' Their apprehension was merited, for an extremely ugly affair erupted in the port city of Tampico before the fires that had ravaged Zacatecas had time to cool.

A band of some hundred and fifty motley adventurers, American and Mexican alike, convening haphazardly in New Orleans, concocted the idea of renting the schooner *Mary Jane* and sailing across the Gulf of Mexico to the post of Tampico, where freedom-loving Mexicans would be sure to join them in a revolt against the murderous tyranny represented by Santa Anna's sack of Zacatecas. It was a harebrained scheme, destined to failure from the moment the poorly navigated *Mary Jane* piled up on a sand bar at the entrance to Tampico harbor.

The accomplices ashore, relying upon help from the men now immobilized aboard the schooner, commenced their battle cries so prematurely that the local garrison had no difficulty in putting down the rebellion. Thirty-one of the would-be invaders were captured by the Mexican forces; three wounded men died, the other twenty-eight were lined up and shot. Frightened by the conjunction of Zacatecas and Tampico, the central government hastily enacted a draconian decree, the law of December 1835: Foreigners who invaded the soil of Mexico and took up arms against Mexico would, if captured, be summarily shot. Within half a year, application of this harsh law at the little Tejas settlement of Goliad would have devastating consequences.

Chapter 7

The Raven Stakes Out
Its Territory

 WHEN DID SAM HOUSTON FIRST EXpress a personal interest in Tejas? Like most informed Americans, especially those from the west, he must have been vaguely aware of developments there, following them occasionally, ignoring them most of the time. He was probably unaware of the Battle of Medina in 1813, for he was then engaged in fighting the Creek Indians in Alabama. In 1822, when Houston was twentynine, he did speculate in Tejas lands, but only as an investor in a tenuous real estate scheme; he was interested in making a quick dollar and not in settlement.

However, on the evening in 1829 when he fled Tennessee in disgrace, while standing on the deck of the boat carrying him down river

113

to lifelong exile from the state he loved, something happened that would eventually head him in that direction:

> I was in an agony of despair and strongly tempted to leap overboard and end my worthless life. At that moment, however, an eagle swooped down near my head, and then, soaring aloft with the wildest screams, was lost in the rays of the setting sun. I knew then that a great destiny waited for me in the West.

Despite this omen, he remained with his Indian friends for three years before a combination of circumstances forced him to consider his future. His old restlessness returned. His vanity was wounded when he suffered defeat in an election to the Cherokee Council. And he had an insatiable yearning to lead men, either in politics or in battle, a predisposition reinforced when he watched his hero, General Jackson. Despite these urgings, he might have remained a heavy drinker lost in the wilderness had not a dramatic affair catapulted him back to the very center of national consciousness.

Whenever through his long life he faced a difficult decision or needed time to get his ideas straightened out, he liked to find himself a stout piece of wood for whittling, and many of

"It was as if two powerful birds had entered the sky within a single year. The Eagle in the south, The Raven in the north..."
—James A. Michener

Santa Ana

Sam Houston

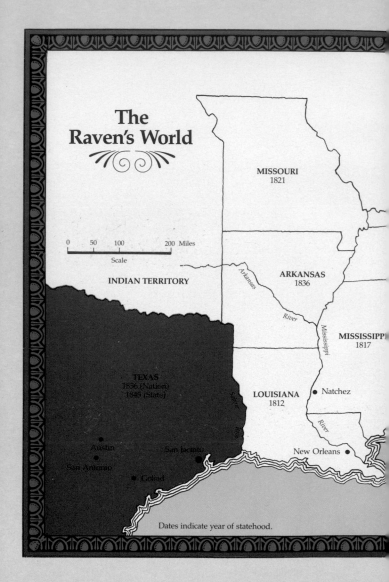

The Raven's World

0 50 100   200 Miles

Scale

INDIAN TERRITORY

MISSOURI
1821

ARKANSAS
1836

MISSISSIPPI
1817

TEXAS
1836 (Nation)
1845 (State)

LOUISIANA
1812

• Austin

• San Jacinto

• San Antonio

• Goliad

Arkansas

River

Mississippi

Sabine

River

• Natchez

New Orleans •

Dates indicate year of statehood.

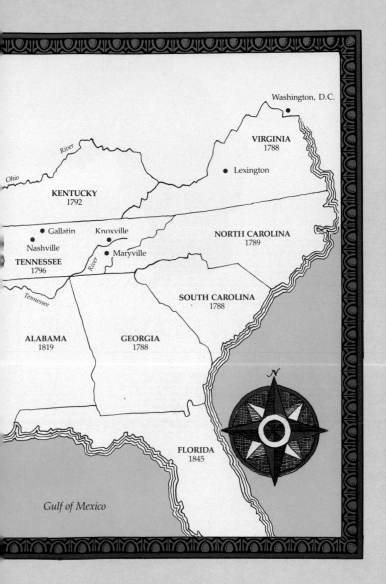

Washington, D.C.

VIRGINIA
1788

Lexington

River

Ohio

KENTUCKY
1792

NORTH CAROLINA
1789

Gallatin   Knoxville

Nashville

Maryville

River

TENNESSEE
1796

SOUTH CAROLINA
1788

Tennessee

ALABAMA
1819

GEORGIA
1788

N

FLORIDA
1845

Gulf of Mexico

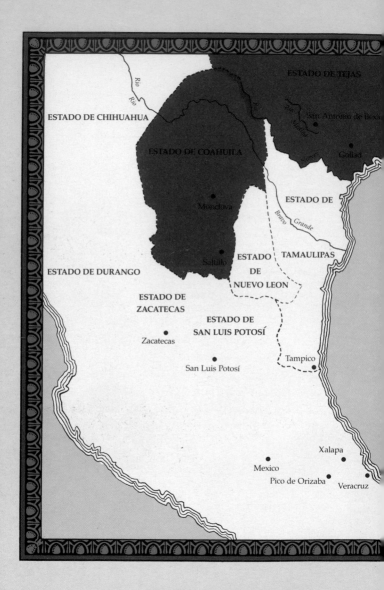

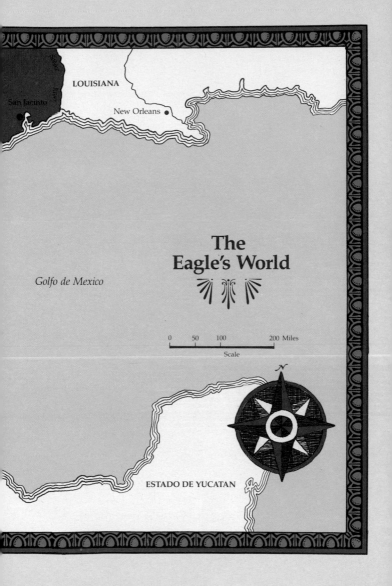

LOUISIANA

San Jacinto

New Orleans •

The
Eagle's World

Golfo de Mexico

0   50   100   200 Miles
Scale

N

ESTADO DE YUCATAN

The Battle of San Jacinto, by H.A. McArdle

James A. Michener

his friends kept as keepsakes ingenious toys and tools he had whittled for them. In January 1832 while passing through Nashville on Indian business, he had searched for an appropriate sapling, cut it down and whittled himself a stout walking stick, which he carried thereafter. Because he was a big man it was a big stick, 'a hefty hunk of hickory', a friend called it. In Washington as a private citizen defending Indian interests, he was carrying it along the streets one night when he came upon Congressman William Stanbery of Ohio, a legislator who had disparaged him on the floor of the House.

Swinging his cudgel with maximum effect, Houston knocked the smaller man to the sidewalk, pummeled him some more, then jumped on him to complete the job. Congressman Stanbery drew a pistol, held it against Houston's breast and pulled the trigger. The gun did not fire, and Houston continued to club the congressman, nearly killing him.

The rules of Congress were severe for such an offense—an attack on a legislator for a speech made within the halls of government; hooliganism like this could not be permitted. Despite the expressed wish of President Jackson that Houston not be disciplined and against the efforts of Congressman James K. Polk of Tennessee to prevent censure, the House voted by an overwhelming majority to try its former member Sam Houston of the Ninth Tennessee

District for having assaulted a former colleague who was still on active service as a congressman.

The Houston trial attracted an enormous amount of attention in Washington, and continued to do so for a month. Houston, in real danger of a prison term if the House trial led to a civil one, hired the best lawyer available, Francis Scott Key of Baltimore, already famous for having written the national anthem.

Key's rather shaky defense was that Houston had indeed chastised Congressman Stanbery, but not because of anything the congressman had said on the floor of the House. Rather, the defendant had belted him over the head several times with a stout hickory stick only because of what newspapers had reported as Stanbery's expressions outside the House.

Oratory for and against Houston was florid; his name dominated the newspapers of the nation; and he became a whipping boy diverting attacks from the administration. His old friend Jackson rallied strongly to his support. It was a circus such as only a young republic could provide, and the ringmaster was Sam Houston. Once again an actor with the Congress his stage, he converted the occasion into a tribute for his past services to the nation rather than a censure for his recent behavior.

His speech in defense of his record was vintage Houston. He prepared for it by getting blind drunk the night before, but once on his feet he was scintillating, referring to Greece,

Rome, Cromwell, the Tsar, Blackstone, and the Apostle Paul. In his peroration he extolled honor and liberty. Bouquets were tossed at his feet, the applause was thunderous, and one woman cried: 'I had rather be Sam Houston in a dungeon than Stanbery on a throne.'

Despite his oratory he was found guilty, but by a much narrower margin than the earlier vote indicting him. The Speaker of the House, a drinking companion the night before the speech, was ordered to reprimand him, which he did on 14 May 1832 in one brief, courteous sentence.

As Houston himself characterized this affair: 'I was dying out, and had they taken me before a Justice of the Peace and fined me ten dollars they would have killed me; but they gave me a national tribunal for a theater and that set me up again.' The former actor had remembered how to act.

Congressman Stanbery, bitter over this gross miscarriage of justice, hauled Houston into civil court on a warrant charging criminal assault, but the case wandered on pretty much in secret until Sam was found guilty of simple assault and fined five hundred dollars, which was later remitted by President Jackson. Since very few people even knew that the trial had been held, Sam was allowed to remain a national hero.

It seems likely that during his enforced stay in Washington to attend his two trials he discussed with his mentor, President Jackson, the situation in Tejas. The facts were complicated. Following the discovery of North America, France led explorations and gained possession of the Mississippi valley while Spain's explorations out of Mexico had established claims to all the areas farther west. In 1762, as a consequence of European wars, France surrendered its vast Louisiana Territory to Spain, which thus completed its claim to most of America west of a vague line' near the great river.

Napoleon, by 1803 so powerful he had been able to force Spain to cede Louisiana back to France, became so preoccupied in Europe that, disgusted by the defeat of his army in Haiti, he decided in a fit of pique to dispose of all remaining French properties in North America. When he offered them to the new United States, Thomas Jefferson leaped at the opportunity to purchase Louisiana and the unmapped lands to the west. At the time of sale, however, no one knew where the boundaries of the property were, so no firm line between Spanish and American holdings could be delineated. For the next sixteen years, 1803–1819, friction along the shadowy line threatened to lead to actual war between the United States and Spain.

The difficulty was understandable. Feisty American hunters, trappers, and traders who operated along the Louisiana frontier, wherever that might be, looked longingly at the rich, empty plains of Spain's northern Mexico, seeking persistently to push westward into Tejas, while Mexicans tried to push their claims as far east as possible. The inevitable result was a contested no-man's strip of land soon occupied by criminals, adventurers, smugglers, and a few honest settlers seeking legitimate land grants.

Something had to be done lest the friction lead to war. In a judicious treaty between Spain and the United States in 1821, Florida was ceded to the United States while the Louisiana-Tejas border was delineated generally in favor of Spain, which meant that Mexico profited. A line of demarcation was drawn along the Sabine River establishing the eastern border of Mexico, and along the Red River defining the northern. Although decisive, it was probably unrealistic, for the American representative, relying upon faulty maps, gave away land he had never seen and did not understand, land which should have been retained by the United States as part of Louisiana. Further negotiations with Mexico were undertaken to push the boundary westward, to no avail. Eventually the Texicans were to resolve the issue—by force of arms.

There was one further complication for the United States. Tejas was being filled with immigrants from states like Tennessee, Alabama, and Mississippi, and settlers from those areas tended to defend slavery whether or not they themselves had any slaves. So if Tejas were to be wrenched from Mexico and brought into the Union, it would probably come bringing two slave senators and perhaps as many as three representatives, upsetting the precarious balance between slave and free in the Congress.

Among the fiercest northern opponents of slavery was John Quincy Adams, who had arranged the treaty that gave the United States Florida, and Spain the advantage along the Louisiana-Tejas border. As a leader hoping to preserve the peace his treaty had initiated, he became suspicious of men like President Jackson and his crony Sam Houston whom he suspected—unfairly in Jackson's case at least—of trying to foment military actions that might lead to war and the incorporation of Tejas into the American union. He thus had ample reason to oppose any Houston adventuring that might provoke war and create a new American slave state or cluster of states from the land which had been Tejas.

It seemed at times that Adams did everything he could to favor Mexico and discredit Texas. He was a stubborn man, the only U.S. ex-president humble enough to slip back into the relative obscurity of the House of Representatives,* becoming in his later years one of its most effective members.

---

*The seventeenth president, Andrew Johnson (1865–1869), after surviving an impeachment re-

In addition to Adams, Houston had a second life-long opponent in the tenacious John C. Calhoun, the longtime Senator from South Carolina whom he had offended over Cherokee matters when Calhoun served as secretary of war. The two men bristled whenever they met.

Houston's third mortal, though still undeclared, enemy was continuing to gather strength. Down in Mexico General Santa Anna was taking those steps which would eventually bring him into conflict with Houston.

The history of 1832–1845 was a record of battle among these powerful men. Santa Anna was the cleverest, the most unprincipled, and in many ways the best brawler. Anyone who opposed this man had better look sharp, or the doughty Mexican would cut the ground away. Calhoun was the most intelligent, without question. Adams had the most resolute moral courage, but he was purblind, stubborn, and in many instances his own worst enemy. Sam Houston was the most honorable and perhaps the most sagacious, but at the same time devious, willing to wait, to surrender one position after another so long as his main target was kept in sight, and to lose small battles while planning for the jugular victory.

All four men lost many battles as good men

---

turned in 1875 to the Senate in which he had served earlier (1857–1862).

will, and all gained immortal victories as persistent men do.

We know that in 1832 Houston once more speculated in Tejas lands, an acceptable practice since George Washington and most of the signers of the Declaration of Independence had speculated in western lands. He also became a legal agent of some kind for the Galveston Bay and Texas Land Company (which would bring financial loss to hundreds of would-be settlers.) So his interest in the area was not trivial.

In December 1832 he entered Tejas for the first time, carrying a passport which gave his height as six-feet-two, even though he claimed at least six-feet-four. He came as a lawyer with a dual commission, one openly avowed, the other secret. As a representative of his Cherokee Indians he rode all the way to San Antonio to meet with the warlike Comanche Indians with whom he sought a truce; as an agent for President Jackson he came to investigate the local political situation and to report on the likelihood of rebellion against the government of Mexico.

It seems likely that Houston, at an early time, foresaw the possibility of rebellion; it seems unquestionable that President Jackson refused to encourage or support it.

However, prospects in Tejas looked promising for a man like Houston, willing to take the risks entailed in fishing troubled waters, so he concluded his Indian affairs and applied for land in Tejas. Elias Rector, an official with excellent reputation, later swore that this conversation took place on Houston's departure:

> ***Elias Rector:*** Houston, I wish to give you something before we separate and I have nothing that will do as a gift except my razor.

> ***Sam Houston:*** Rector, I accept your gift, and mark my words, if I have luck this razor will some day shave the chin of a president of the republic.

Others who heard Rector report the conversation immediately after it was supposed to have taken place testified that the final response was slightly more grandiose:

> ***Sam Houston:*** Elias, remember my words. I will yet be the president of a great republic. I will bring that nation to the United States, and if they don't watch me closely I will be the president of the White House yet.

In 1833 he arrived in Nacogdoches, took up temporary residence and even represented the area in a constitutional convention, where he performed as a sober, responsible voice preaching caution. There was rumor that he sent back to Arkansas for his Indian wife, Tiana Rogers, but she did not join him and thus passes from history. (Until the arrival of a later member of her distinguished Cherokee family, the political humorist, Will Rogers.)

His taste of Tejas life was apparently not heady enough to make Houston want to stay in the turbulent area permanently, for the end of 1833 saw him back among his Cherokee friends. In 1834, however, he returned to Mexico so determined to own more land that he was willing to convert to Catholicism to obtain it, a prudent rather than a spiritual decision.

Decades previously, when the Mexican government watched the first groups of Americans come streaming into Tejas with Protestant affiliations, the government had passed a law which would protect the Catholic religion: 'If you want free land here, you must convert.' Three of the prominent Americans in Tejas, Stephen Austin its founder, Jim Bowie its defender, and Sam Houston its leader, were accused by their neighbors of converting only to obtain land. The first two did so seriously, but Houston with fingers crossed. As soon as he received his land Houston apparently reverted to the stern Protestantism of Tennessee.

It was now that Houston wrote two important letters which give evidence of his ability to make sober estimates of complex situations. In one of the letters he made four shrewd observations: (1) The situation in Tejas cannot remain as it is now. (2) Tejas will not be acquired by the United States during the administration of General Jackson, for his sense of honor will not permit this. (3) Even if Tejas were acquired by treaty, the present Senate would not allow its admission as a state because of the slavery problem. (4) Tejas must look to herself and do for herself, and within a year she will produce events of importance to her future and beneficial to her prosperity.

In the other letter Houston even more bluntly predicted that within one year Tejas would be a sovereign state within the Mexican system, and within three it would be separated from Mexico and would remain so forever.

His observations displayed extraordinary perspicacity and a subtle understanding of both the American and the Mexican mind, but when referring to his own probable future he either guessed wrong or lied, for in the same letters he added this contradictory note:

> Many suppose that such events will be sought by us, but in this their notions will be gratuitous, I assure you! The course that I may pursue, you must rely upon it, shall be for the true interest of Tejas (as I may believe) and if it can be done, as it ought to be; to preserve her integrity to the Confederacy of Mexico.

The fact that he had converted to Mexico's religion and accepted citizenship in that country suggests that his intentions were honorable, at least on the surface, but his behavior in Tejas took him step by irrevocable step toward revolution. At first he claimed only that he was defending the right of Coahuila-y-Tejas, under the Constitution of 1824, to separate into two states, Coahuila south of the Nueces River with Saltillo as its capital, Tejas to the north with San Felipe de Austin or some similar settlement as its capital. He wrote to New Orleans suggesting that volunteers rush into Tejas to speed the break, and he took to issuing wildly provocative calls to duty as well as challenges to Mexican authority. In his predilection for the florid *pronunciamento* he was beginning to resemble Santa Anna, but it is sobering to note that both his and all other such cries from Tejas, after first stressing patriotism and the defense of freedom, always pointed out to listeners that much good land would be their reward for volunteering if they rushed in bringing their guns. Patriotism and profit could move forward in tandem.

Since the American immigrants occupied only a narrow segment of Tejas—the strip of land inward from the Gulf of Mexico—most settlers knew the other families in the area, and Houston now came into contact with four immigrants whose lives were for a few shattering weeks to be intertwined with his in the forging of a new nation.

Jim Bowie, a Tennessee frontier fighter forty years old, had lived in Tejas since 1828 and, after converting to Catholicism, had married into a prestigious Mexican family. His reputation was shadowy and violent: knife fighter with a horrendous twelve-inch blade that now carries his name, alligator-wrestler in the bayous of Louisiana, silver-mine seeker in the desert, operator of a cotton mill in Coahuila, slave runner, landowner, patriot. Volatile and courageous, he did not seek trouble but faced it when it stumbled into his path. He had killed at least one man in a knife duel—and probably several others. His beautiful Mexican wife had died in 1833 after only two years of married life, killed by cholera which swept the area. He was distraught, lonely, and ready for adventure.

Davy Crockett was older than either Houston or Bowie, having been born in Tennessee in 1786. Tall like Houston, he had also served in the Tennessee legislature and for three terms in the national Congress, where he distinguished himself as a Whig who refused to kowtow to the narrow wishes of his constituents or to the dictates of President Jackson, a Democrat. When his fiery independence cost him his seat in Congress, he told the voters: 'You may all go to hell. I'm going to Texas,' and like others of that time who had experienced defeat, he lit out for the wild adventures then available in Tejas, abandoning his family. He arrived with a reverberating reputation as a frontiersman, having fought Indians throughout the southeast and claiming to have killed more than a hundred bear in one eight-month period. He crossed the border into Tejas the last day of December 1835.

William Travis was youngest of the four, only twenty-six years old, a moody, disorganized lawyer from South Carolina. Like Davy Crockett, he had abandoned his wife and children, but in his case there were extenuating circumstances. He seems not to have fled his small town in Alabama willingly; he killed a man who was reputed to be his wife's lover. Her second child, a girl born after Travis left, was probably the child of some other man. At any rate, he arrived in Tejas alone in 1831, announcing in one sworn statement that he was single, later that he was a widower. When his wife tried to effect a reconciliation, he spurned her and instead sought a divorce. Bellicose, temperamental, brave, he received a commission in the informal rebellious army and volunteered his services to General Houston, who recognized him as a man difficult to discipline but splendid to rely upon in time of real trouble. A man with a troubled background, Travis would, as he faced death, write one of the noblest letters of American history, a communication whose splendid words would echo throughout Texas for all time.

James Walker Fannin, Jr., who would become the martyred hero of Goliad, was only thirty-one on the eve of revolution and is unquestionably the most difficult of the four to understand. An appointee to West Point from

Georgia, he quit after two unsatisfactory years but thereafter considered himself a military genius. Desperate for money, he had earlier, like Jim Bowie, run African slaves illegally from Cuba to Georgia to Tejas. When he immigrated to Tejas in 1834 he brought his wife and two daughters with him. Extraordinarily vain, he hoped to become commanding general of the rebellion. When this was denied him, however, and Sam Houston was elected by the provisional Tejas government to command the army, he bit his lip and proved unusually energetic in whatever job was given him, appointing himself a one-man committee of correspondence in an attempt to enlist West Pointers to the cause. He was demonstrably brave and not loath to strike out on his own. He was a capable, if sometimes confused, leader.

There were many such volatile American spirits in Tejas in the closing months of 1835, most of them residents of the Mexican state for only a few years, and in some cases a few months or even weeks. The attitudes held between them and the other contending parties, the natives of Mexico, would color their relationships. Mexicans, especially the *peninsulares* born in Spain and the *criollos* with strong Spanish affinities even though born in Mexico, believed the Americans who had invaded their state of Coahuila-y-Tejas to be lacking in grace, culture and ability. Indeed, the defenders of Spanish glory often described the Americans as unlettered barbarians and infidels asking for chastisement.

Americans also held their adversaries in contempt, clearly expressed in a comparison voiced by a young woman schoolteacher familiar with Tejas:

> The instinct of races never dies out any more than individuals. Anglo-Americans are hardy and enduring beyond all other races. Endowed with an incredible and inexhaustible energy, they never turn back or yield to reverses, however severe or crushing. On the other hand, the modern Mexicans are, as it were, the debris of several inferior and degraded races; African and Indian crossed and mixed, and even the old Spanish blood mixed with the Moorish and demoralized by a long course of indolence and political corruption; both physically and mentally they are the very antithesis of the Anglo-American. They are weak as he is strong; they run where he fights.

It was going to shock these over-confident Americans when they found that the despised Mexicans would win the first military encounters. General Santa Anna and his supporting officers knew how to fight and how to win. The Americans would win only one major battle, the one that counted, the last one.

It was apparent to President Santa Anna, as leader of Mexico, that some dramatic action was needed to bring these obstreperous Yankees to their senses, so he dispatched his young brother-in-law, General Martín Cós, to San Antonio de Béxar to discipline them.

With great fanfare General Cós, who seems to have been just another routine officer elevated to high office by nepotism, marched north with a military commission which also entitled him to serve as civil governor. He found he would first have to settle a dispute between two cities, each of which claimed to be the capital of the huge state; Saltillo backed Santa Anna's position of a strong central government but nearby Monclova defended the concept of state's rights. Cós naturally sided with his relative, Santa Anna.

Forced to use the army to settle the affair in Saltillo's favor, Cós then left Coahuila and proceeded toward Tejas, the northern part of the hyphenated state, announcing that he would expel all Americans who had infiltrated the area since 1830. This would include Houston, Travis, and Fannin, and men like Crockett who had not yet come across the border. Furthermore he was going to arrest all federalists suspected of opposing the imposition of the new centralist constitution. Judging from what had happened in Zacatecas and Tampico, these would be shot.

General Cós seemed well on his way to subduing the incipient rebellion without aid from his brother-in-law, but at Béxar an informal collection of tough-minded local citizens rallied and, with a superb sense of military deportment which ought to have alerted the Mexican leadership as to the possible qualities of the other settlers, drove Cós not only out of Béxar but out of Tejas as well.

Historians have not been able to unravel the resultant confusion. The victorious Texicans, as they were beginning to call themselves, allowed Cós and his troops to march south unmolested because the Mexican officers had given solemn promise—some say in writing— to leave Tejas. That much is clear. But the Texicans later claimed the Mexicans had also promised that they would never return to take arms against the settlers, who at this point in late 1835 wanted only a separate state of their own not associated with Coahuila, and the right to all freedoms guaranteed by the Constitution of 1824.

This Santa Anna could not grant. Nor could he honor his brother-in-law's pledge never again to fight against the Tejanos. 'To hell with vague promises!' Santa Anna cried. 'Your men will join my army. We will invade Tejas and put it to the sword.' And with this terrible intention he prepared to march north to his con-

frontation with General Houston, frontiersman Davy Crockett, brooding William Travis, would-be general, James Fannin, and knife-wielding Jim Bowie, a Mexican citizen of good standing.

Chapter 8

The Eagle Strikes

 As a reward for his rape of Zacatecas, President Santa Anna had been promoted to the rank of general-in-chief and given the exalted title *Benemérito en Grado Heroico*, and there was a rumor that if he succeeded in subduing the Tejanos he was to be named *Benemérito Universal y Perpetuo*.

Accordingly, he spent the late fall of 1835 preparing his army for a major assault against those infuriating dissidents who had begun calling themselves Texicans. Almost none of the Anglos had been born in Tejas and many had been there for less than a year. He agreed with an aide who assured him: 'They're little better than that rabble you helped defeat at Medina in 1813. Cutthroats sprung from Amer-

139

ican jails, adventurers who drift down the Mississippi River, corrupt traders from Louisiana, and, I will admit, a few honest farmers from Kentucky, Tennessee, and Alabama.'

What particularly infuriated Santa Anna was the surprising number of settlers with Spanish names who sided with the Anglos, sensible and well-educated men like Lorenzo de Zavala, who had been his close friend during the liberal days, then a prisoner for three years in San Juan de Ulúa in Veracruz Bay, delegate to the *cortes* in Spain, a member of the senate, minister to France, and governor of the State of Mexico. One of the wisest and grandest of contemporary Mexicans, he had found Santa Anna's violation of the Constitution of 1824 unacceptable and had fled north to Tejas to join the rebels.

What was such a man, Santa Anna wanted to know, yelping about? There were others like him, and the dictator was determined to capture and shoot them all. He had developed the simplistic idea that anyone who failed to follow his mercurial shifts deserved to be eliminated: 'I will set directions, and men like Zavala are obligated to leap into line.'

Often during that critical year of preparation Santa Anna reminded his subordinates: 'Zacatecas was only a beginning,' and he indicated on the map the towns he would annihilate in the coming battle: 'San Antonio de Béxar, Nacogdoches, San Felipe de Austin, Victoria . . . all must feel our fury.'

140

Because the Mexican army would play a key role in the forthcoming invasion, its unique composition must be understood. It was a large conscript army of untrained, illiterate, and un-uniformed peasants clustered about a well-drilled professional officer corps. The middle-rank officers were first class; the foot-soldiers were cannon fodder. The cavalry was the best in the New World; the artillery was pathetic. The field generals were an uncertain lot; some were almost as skilled as Santa Anna but the bulk were incompetent opportunists who used the army as their gold mine. Services like the medical corps, the engineers, and logistics were abominable, if they existed at all. But one fact became apparent in all the engagements this army undertook: some of the officers and men were among the bravest to be found anywhere, accounting for the many victories the Mexican forces won.

The Mexican army operated under difficulties. Since the central government was continually bankrupt, the generals had to borrow money from lenders who charged forty-eight percent per annum. Deliveries of guns that would not fire and food that could not be eaten were common. One large sum, turned over to Santa Anna's son-in-law for the purchase of supplies, largely vanished; he stole it. One general sold supplies to his own troops at outrageous prices; another lent money he had sequestered during previous campaigns at four percent per month. There were no doctors and no priests to give last rites to men who sometimes died at shocking rates, even from ordinary illnesses that could have been cured.

When Santa Anna left the capital to take command of the Army of Operations, as it was technically called, he supposed that he would find thirty thousand trained professional troops awaiting him; he found two thousand, the others having deserted. To repair the deficiency he ordered mass levies, sweeps through the countryside that resulted in impressment, the opening of jails, and the gathering up of illiterates and incompetents. From the Yucatán and the peninsula below Oaxaca, huge formations of white trousered, sandaled Indians, who had never known cold or seen snow were marched north without even knowing the language under which they were to serve.

It was a sprawling mass that greeted Santa Anna, and its miraculous conversion into a fighting force was possible only through his military expertise. An aide said: 'He commands everything. He is a cavalryman, footsoldier, commissary, priest, map maker, artilleryman, and drill master. If we had three others like him we could conquer the world.' Santa Anna himself had threatened: 'If those Americans give me trouble, I may march right on and capture Washington.'

The officers of Santa Anna's army, when properly accoutered, were a handsome lot, especially the cavalry, which wore blue trousers adorned by a scarlet side-seam, a scarlet pigeon-tailed jacket with green lapels and epaulets, and a green collar. The cap was of tanned cowhide with a high wooden plume which remained erect even during a charge; distinction was provided by the crossed white straps of the bandoleer. The horses, too, were caparisoned in blazing colors.

But the predominant look of the Mexican army was determined by the infantry, which was supposed to wear white trousers, blue jackets with scarlet cuffs and front edging, and green epaulets. This uniform was topped by a tall, black leather hat bearing a red plume, and a big brass shield. Broad white bandoleers crossed the chest, and emphasis was added by the red blanket roll that was carried on the shoulders behind the neck. Properly uniformed infantrymen, well decked out, could evoke memories of Napoleon's armies, obsolete in their flamboyancy but imposing nevertheless.

Unfortunately, because funds for equipment were often stolen by the generals, not one foot soldier in ten had a uniform. Most had to march in the loose white trousers of the countryside, topped by a flimsy white shirt and no hat at all. If they had shoes, and many did not, they were apt to be sandals. The appearance of Santa Anna's army was not what a Prussian drill master would have approved. It looked to be a rabble.

This impression was reinforced by a tradition whereby a soldier's entire family accompanied him on maneuvers in the field and, not infrequently, into battle itself. The women—wives, laundresses, cooks, and prostitutes—marched with their men, as did many children, dressed in whatever rags they happened to find at the moment, creating a messy following often many miles long. Old women, young adventuresses, bawling children, mules and donkeys if the family had any, stoves for the night campfire, and village merchants hoping to make a sale ... all followed the army. A fashion-plate general like Santa Anna rarely galloped back to see how his rear was doing, even a hasty sight of it was repugnant, but the entourage was necessary because the army failed to provide regular food for the men. Had the women not foraged the countryside, their men would have starved.

It was such an army that marched out of the assembly area at Saltillo on 25 January 1836. General Santa Anna and his resplendent staff galloped ahead to Monclova and, by 13 February, Santa Anna was already snug inside the little town far ahead of his troops who were still trying to traverse the exposed and dangerous wasteland north of Saltillo. He worried little about his men because the day started with a comfortable temperature near sixty and became so warm that many soldiers removed their jackets and marched in shirts only, or sometimes not even that. But this was the region that played host to the dreaded blue norther in which, under a leaden sky and the persistent winds of an incoming storm, the temperature could drop thirty or forty degrees in less than half an hour.

Such a storm now hit the unprepared men who had never experienced the phenomenon, and at its first warning blast they quickly donned their shirts and jackets.

Rapidly the temperature dropped to fifty, then forty, then to an appalling thirty. Men began to slow their pace, hugging themselves to keep warm, and mules started to wander in confusion. By mid-afternoon a wild, blinding snowstorm was sweeping across the unfettered prairies of Coahuila-y-Tejas, and at dusk men and animals began to freeze.

All night the dreadful storm continued, throwing twelve to fourteen inches of snow upon men who had never before felt its icy fingers. They began to collapse from frozen fatigue. When the snow covered them they appeared as inert white mounds along the route of the march, as if in their final moments they had pulled a fleecy blanket over their dying bodies.

Worst hit were the pitiful Indians from Yucatán; they simply fell down and died, hundreds of them with no shoes, no blankets, no warm clothing of any kind. Sometimes eight or nine would huddle together in a hopeless mass, clutching one another for even a fragmentary warmth. When they perished the snow formed a rounded hump over them, a kind of natural mausoleum. When more fortunate troops from colder climates, men owning shoes and blankets, spotted such a mound they dug inside, stripped the dead bodies of whatever cloth remained, and wrapped their own bodies and faces against the storm.

At the rear, of course, the women and children suffered terribly. Like the Yucatecs, they huddled in groups, but many died. It was shocking for the rear-guard soldiers who trailed far behind to come upon the frozen bodies of children abandoned in the snow.

Horses, mules, and oxen, also unaccustomed to such a storm, dashed across the blinding landscape, running into trees and collapsing in huge drifts which quickly hid them. When the storm was at its worst, real terror struck—a horde of Apaches, who had long known how to protect themselves during a blue norther, began to ravage the stragglers, stealing what horses remained and what stores of food were still available.

However, an even worse Indian peril awaited, for a new tribe had recently exploded into the region, the fiercest and most capable ever to terrify the west. They were the Comanches, the horse Indians who had galloped down from the mountain regions around Utah to establish themselves firmly in western Tejas. Remorseless in battle, even more cruel than the Apaches when prisoners were taken, they were a swift-riding scourge who would never be controlled, only eliminated, and now one of their raiding parties on its way to plunder Saltillo, a favorite target, saw the Mexican army trapped in the snow and powerless.

In all their western battles the dreaded Comanches never attacked a major force head-on; with curdling battle cries they would parry and thrust at any isolated position. With such tactics they now decimated the entire western perimeter of the hapless army, sweeping in to kill those they could and capturing whatever equipment was left.

When the norther subsided, and the remaining men and mules were counted, Santa Anna's army found it had suffered a tremendous loss. The general, safe inside stout walls, must have been aware of the disaster, but neither then nor ever did he refer to it. He believed that an army must accept casualties when required to march over great distances, a reality of war, unpleasant but acceptable.

And from the practical point of view, the army's experience in the Monclova blizzard may have been salutary, for it got rid of the largely useless Yucatecs, it toughened up the line, and it enabled one young lieutenant who dreamed of impending glory to tell his mates: 'If we can survive that blizzard and those Comanches, we have little to fear from the rebels in Tejas. It'll be Zacatecas all over again.'

Joining his now depleted army, General Santa Anna continued his advance north into Tejas where he directed his army, still huge, toward San Antonio. There, in an old mission building, the Americans who had filtered into

Tejas waited to defend what they were already thinking of as 'our new nation.'

The Alamo, a name probably derived from a nearby grove of cottonwood trees, had originally been founded in 1718 as the San Antonio de Valero Mission. In the years since the chapel's cornerstone was laid in 1744, the building had acquired sturdy, protective, fortress-like walls and, in fact, was used as a barracks building for Mexican soldiers after the mission was abandoned in 1797. Now these walls protected Davy Crockett, Jim Bowie, and William B. Travis, who were extremely brave but who commanded only 184 other defenders, including some dozen native Mexicans who had chosen to fight alongside the Americans. Since Santa Anna had more than five thousand soldiers in his attacking force, a Mexican victory seemed inevitable.

For thirteen relentless days the Mexican troops besieged the defenders of the Alamo. Santa Anna conducted the battle under a blood-red flag to the marching tune *Degüello*, each symbol traditionally meaning: 'Surrender now or you will be executed when we win.' In the final charge through the walls of the Alamo there would be no quarter; the men inside knew that this time the often windy cry 'Victory or Death' meant what it said.

Early in the morning of the thirteenth day Santa Anna's foot soldiers, lashed forward by officers who did not care how many of their men were lost in the attack, stormed the walls, overcame the defenders, and slaughtered every man inside, American or Mexican. Jim Bowie was slain in his sick bed. Captain Travis was shot on the walls. What exactly happened to Davy Crockett would never be known—dead inside the walls or murdered later outside as a prisoner of war. But dead.

The Texicans lost 186, the Mexicans about 600. One Texican, a grizzled French veteran of the Napoleonic wars, had fled the fort before the last fight began. Santa Anna had won a crushing victory and had been remorseless in exterminating Texicans.

Any evaluation of Mexico's stunning victory at the Alamo must consider two hideous acts of Santa Anna, acts so contemptuous of the customary decencies which always existed between honorable adversaries that they enraged the Americans, kindling fires of revenge that would be extinguished only in the equally horrible acts that followed the great Tejas victory at San Jacinto. When a group of prisoners was brought to Santa Anna he said scornfully: 'I do not want to see those men living' and despite the rules which ensured safety to soldiers who surrendered honorably, he growled: 'Shoot them,' and they were executed.

Enraging the Texicans even more was his treatment of the bodies of the men who had died bravely trying to defend the Alamo. Instead of providing the bodies with a decent burial, or turning them over to their friends for proper burial, he had the corpses thrown into a great pile, as if they were useless timbers, then cremated in slow fires for two and a half days. When the heat subsided, scavenging citizens probed the ashes for metal items of value, after which the bones were left to dogs and vultures. When news of the desecration circulated, a fearful oath was sworn by Texicans: 'Remember the Alamo!'

Flushed by his triumph, Santa Anna behaved as if he were all-powerful. When a detachment of his army won a second victory at Goliad, some miles southeast of San Antonio, taking more than four hundred prisoners during several skirmishes, he ordered the general in charge to execute every man. The general reminded Santa Anna by messenger that he had persuaded the Texicans, many of them volunteers who had been in Tejas less than six months, to surrender by guaranteeing their personal safety and granting them full honors of war: 'I pledged my word to treat them honorably and am bound to do so. I must with due respect refuse to execute them while they are unarmed and under my protection.'

When Santa Anna received this message he broke into a rage: 'Has he not heard of that law we passed last year after the American invasion at Tampico? It orders the immediate execution of any foreigner invading our sacred land with evil intent.' Using the same messenger who had brought him news of refusal, he dispatched a harsh rebuke to the general holding the prisoners at Goliad: 'I therefore order, that you should give immediate effect to the said ordinance in respect to all those foreigners who have the audacity to come and insult the republic . . . I trust you will inform me that public vengeance has been satisfied by the punishment of such detestable delinquents.' In simple words: 'Execute the rebels.'

On a bright spring morning, the Mexicans marched nearly four hundred unarmed prisoners in three different groups along country roads, suddenly turning on them and murdering three hundred and forty-two. Those who escaped by fleeing across fields, ducking into woods, and throwing themselves into streams in which they swam to safety, spread news of the massacre. Across Texas men whispered with a terrifying lust for vengeance: 'Remember the Alamo! Remember Goliad!'

By design, Sam Houston had missed both encounters. Like Quintus Fabius Maximus, he preferred to gather men and weapons, waiting for a time and a location more favorable to his cause. The Eagle and The Raven were almost ready for their great confrontation. In the wintry days of 1836 they circled ever closer, preparing for the battle which would determine the outcome of the war and the future of Texas.

Chapter 9

San Jacinto—
Raven and Eagle At War

 At last The Eagle and The Raven were to meet, in a swampy area between two rivulets at a place called San Jacinto in the Mexican state of Coahuila-y-Tejas. For more than forty years, unknowingly, each had been preparing himself for this historic confrontation. Even though neither approached it unsullied or with any guarantee of success, the future of two great nations depended upon its outcome.

Although Santa Anna had won every engagement so far, he had not succeeded in driving the Texicans from the field. Houston, by adroit maneuvering described by his political enemies as cowardice, had lured Santa Anna far north of his supply depots. Finally the two adversaries faced one another along the banks of the little San Jacinto River, nine hundred Texicans facing about twelve hundred and fifty battle-hardened but exhausted Mexicans.

Prospects for Houston were not bright, but in the late afternoon of 21 April 1836, when the sun was low and shining in Mexican eyes, he was provided a lucky break. Santa Anna, convinced that the Texicans would not dare to attack at that late hour when they were so badly outnumbered, had retired to his tent for a siesta, perhaps made somnolent by the warm weather, a heavy meal, and a soupçon of opium.* With their general thus engaged, no one on the Mexican side attended to the duties of warfare: guards were not posted nor picket lines manned nor buglers on watch.

Striking with terrible force, the Texicans thundered directly into the Mexican lines. Signals were not flashed back to Santa Anna's headquarters, nor were any staff there to receive them if they had been sent. In those first moments of battle, the outcome was decided. Before the Mexicans could rally, Houston's men were rampaging through the lines, creating havoc and dealing death. When the pan-

---

*Persistent legend claims that he was dallying with Emily Morgan, a beautiful mulatto girl perhaps immortalized in song and history as the Yellow Rose of Texas. Many doubt her role in the siesta.

icking troops sought safety in a nearby swamp, the Texicans rushed after them, fighting waist deep in the bayou waters, shooting them in the back and sometimes grabbing the Mexicans by the hair, jerking their heads backward and slashing their throats with long knives .

Mexicans who knew they were about to die screamed: 'Me no Alamo!' Me no Goliad!' but the slaughter continued. At the height of the massacre, General Houston, unlike his opponent Santa Anna who didn't understand the conventions of warfare, shouted at his rampaging men: 'Gentleman, gentlemen!' followed by a plea that they not kill the Mexicans but take them prisoner. When he rode on, one of his captains lingered to issue an order which one soldier later reported as: 'Boys, you know how to take prisoners, take them with the butt of yor guns & remember the Alamo, remember Goliad & club right and left, and nock their god damn brains out!' The battle lasted only eighteen minutes but was so furious that, when it ended, more than six hundred Mexicans lay dead on the battlefield and in the swampy waters of the bayou, and another six hundred were taken captive. Only three Texicans lost their lives, but in the days that followed seven others would die from wounds.

In those eighteen explosive minutes, some of the most fateful in American history, Sam Houston and his revenge-seeking Texicans rerouted the development of North America. Temporarily Texas would become a free nation subservient to no other government. In time, the areas of New Mexico, Arizona, and California would also be torn away from Mexico and become American states. The map would be forever altered.

In this great battle involving few soldiers but massive consequences, how did our two adversaries conduct themselves? Sam Houston, after a vacillating indecision as to whether or not to fight, heroically threw himself and his men against considerable odds. Twice his horse was shot out from under him and a bullet shattered his ankle.

Santa Anna, on the other hand, dashed from his tent, saw all was lost, grabbed a pair of trousers and escaped from the blood-soaked battlefield. Determined to stay alive, he protected himself through that first night by moving silently about and keeping away from everyone. When the sun rose, a detachment of six Texicans probing the areas around the battle site for more prisoners detected a lone man standing in an open prairie and surrounded him. He surrendered peacefully but denied he was an officer: 'We then inquired of him if he knew where Santa Anna was. To which he replied that he did not.'

Disappointed at having captured a mere foot soldier and angry at the captive's slow movement because his feet were unaccustomed to walking, one of the Texicans volunteered to shoot him. Others protested and Santa Anna might have escaped undetected had not Mexican soldiers begun calling out '¡*Presidente!*' when the disheveled prisoner was dragged into the camp.

In the commotion that followed, the Mexican was hauled with pistols at his head before Sam Houston who lay stretched on the ground under the branches of a huge tree, his badly wounded right leg swathed in bloody bandages. Meeting each other at last, the two antagonists spent the first moments making unspoken decisions of the greatest significance to Mexico and Texas.

Neither soldier revealed his strategy at that moment, but later events proved that each had been at the top of his wits in this historic encounter. Santa Anna's priorities were simple: 'Stay alive. Tell them anything. Do anything. Promise anything. Just stay alive.' To start the meeting in his favor, he first humiliated himself, bowing slightly to the victor, but then he became the quintessential Santa Anna. Hauling himself erect and assuming a military pose he spoke grandiloquently in words that others heard and recorded: 'Mi General, ha derrotado el Napoleón del oeste!' (You have defeated the Napoleon of the West.) When some of the Texicans who understood Spanish snickered, a Mexican officer from a good family said in English: 'That one has fought more battles than Napoleon and Washington combined.' There was a muttered demand among some Texicans that he be summarily shot because of the horrors of Alamo and Goliad, but

Houston resisted, for his mind was galloping along with but one goal before it: 'Save Texas. To hell with revenge. I ought to strangle this Mexican for what he did to our men at the Alamo and Goliad. And the men certainly want to shoot him, but if I can keep him alive, he can be used.'

So Santa Anna's life was spared. Houston's lookouts had returned to camp with alarming news: 'General Filisola has at least seven thousand Mexican troops not far away on the Brazos. Other substantial Mexican armies are massed farther south and may strike at any time.' And from his own observations he knew that his fledgling nation of Texas was a fragile affair which could not withstand extended warfare. With the political sagacity that had always marked him, Houston maneuvered Santa Anna into signing a cease fire which immobilized the other Mexican forces and provided the new-born nation of Texas breathing space in which to consolidate its free existence. It was a masterful stroke.

But what happened to Santa Anna, this discredited Napoleon who had, through negligence, lost his army? After Houston spared his life and used him to defuse the Mexican armies, he treated the Mexican with a generosity Santa Anna admitted he could hardly have hoped for. Houston, abiding by the rules of civilized warfare, gave his enemy a solemn pledge: 'General, I give you my word of honor that you will not be molested or harmed.' The new-world Napoleon was to benefit from the old-world military code of honor which he himself had violated so hideously after his victories at the Alamo and Goliad, but Houston's pledge was ignored when he had to leave camp to receive medical treatment for his shattered ankle. Houston's second-in-command, less forgiving and lenient, threw Santa Anna into prison in chains and kept him there for fifty-two days. Undaunted and while still a prisoner of the Texans as they now called themselves, he paraded his insouciance and became the conniving bounder he had always been. When Houston returned, his leg cured, Santa Anna started talking fast, making gargantuan promises, and persuading Houston, even over the objections of the Texas legislature, to set him free as an ambassador of good will between the two warring nations. Then he beguiled the Mexican consul in New Orleans to provide funds which would enable him to travel, not back to Mexico City but north to Washington, where he became the sensation of the moment, arguing Mexico's case with the American president and senators.

Nothing reveals the duplicity of Santa Anna more strikingly than the farewell speech he made to the Texicans who had captured and treated him far more decently than he had treated his prisoners: 'My friends! I have been a witness to your courage in the field of battle. Rely with confidence on my sincerity, and you shall never have cause to regret the kindness

shown me. In returning to my native land, I beg you to receive the sincere thanks of your grateful friend. Farewell!'

Despite this catastrophic defeat, the ever-resurgent Santa Anna would return to Mexico in two years to continue his dance with the Mexican presidency, and under his leadership Mexico would suffer even further humiliating defeats.

The postwar record of Houston, however, was brilliant: 1836, first president of Texas; 1841, third president; 1846, first United States Senator from the new state of Texas; 1859, withdrawal from the U.S. Senate to become governor. Despite all the problems of establishing a new nation, he never had any doubts about the prosperous future of Texas, with its rich soils, hardy forests, teeming ocean, and industrious settlers. And in 1840 he finally found happiness in the person of a charming Alabama woman, twenty-six years younger than himself and the daughter of a Baptist preacher. Through her efforts and pleading, Sam was finally baptized a Christian, as were the eight children he and Margaret had.

But then his chain of good luck fractured . . . on the question of slavery. Although most small farmers in Texas owned few or no slaves, the large plantation owners depended heavily upon slave labor. Therefore, Texas was solidly southern in its loyalties and tended to side with those principles that would result in the Confederacy. The slavery problem had been of major concern to Houston during his presidency of the new republic. With the rise in immigration, Houston foresaw that the concurrent rise in the slave population would endanger chances for an eventual annexation of Texas to the United States, a goal he ardently desired. A two-thirds majority of the U.S. Senate could not be mustered for a treaty to annex Texas, but President John Tyler brilliantly proposed instead a congressional joint resolution, which required only a simple majority, and one of his last acts before leaving office in March 1845, was to sign this joint resolution. After the Texas lone star had been added to the national constellation, Houston wrote 'I went into the Senate a national man, and every act of mine, from then on, was as an American statesman with the broadest impress of nationality.'

His dedicated and farsighted concern for the nation as a whole went contrary to the pro-slavery, pro-southern concerns of his constituents, and in 1857 he was defeated in his campaign for governor. In 1859, however, he won his race despite ever-increasing secession sentiment. 'As long as I hold office Texas will remain in the Union,' he said, but as a confirmed believer in democracy he promised that he would yield to any decision of the people. 'But if Texas insists on seceding, I'd rather see her form a separate Republic again rather than join the rest of the South.' Despite fears for his safety, he courageously stumped the state to prevent secession. He suffered no violence, only polite silence. 'It may be that I stand almost alone here in my love for my country, but I yield to no man in my love for Texas.'

Alone he did stand. Even his son was to join the Confederate army after Texas seceded officially in March 1861 with an overwhelming vote of 46,153 to 14,747. In the rebellion that followed, Governor Houston foresaw doom and defeat, but in loyalty to Texas, he reluctantly turned down an offer by President Lincoln to support his endeavor to keep Texas in the Union by landing a large force of Federal troops on the Texas coast. Even when the pro-South sentiment of Texas was so clearly revealed, he attempted to temporize. Rationalizing that whereas he had been directed to take Texas out of the Union, this did not necessarily mean that he had to take it into the Confederacy, he reasoned that Texas should revert to its 1836 status as a free republic, attached to neither the North or South, and as governor he acted accordingly.

This sophistry was not acceptable to the fire-eating pro-South Texans, and in 1861 they kicked him out of the governor's chair so that they might fight on the side of the Confederacy.

At this crisis his friends arranged for a Union military contingent to keep him in office by force, a plan which, if executed, might have succeeded had Houston not had a long history as a patriot in defense of established governments, first in Tennessee, then the Indian nations, the free nation of Texas, and the United States. Refusing to take an oath to support the Confederate States of America or to allow the Union army to keep him in office by force, he surrendered his office in dignity. In his place the Texans installed Lieutenant-Governor Edward Clark, who took the state into the Confederacy as a full partner, and into the ultimate defeat Houston had foreseen.

On the last night, alone in the Executive Chamber he was forced to vacate, Houston sadly wrote:

> 'Fellow citizens . . . I refuse to take this oath. In the name of my own conscience . . . I refuse to take this oath . . . I love Texas too well to bring strife and bloodshed upon her . . . and shall make no endeavor to maintain my authority as chief executive of this State except by peaceful exercise of my functions. When I can no longer do this I shall calmly withdraw, leaving the government in the hands of those who have usurped my authority, but still claiming that I am its chief executive. . . .
>
> It is, perhaps, meet that my career should close thus. I have seen patriots and statesmen of my youth one by one gathered to their fathers, and the government which they have reared rent in twain . . . I stand the last almost of

my race . . . stricken down because I will not yield those principles which I have fought for. . . . The severest pang is that the blow comes in the name of the State of Texas.'

In the middle of the war, Sam Houston retired to his farm where he died in 1863, surrounded by his loving wife and children.

Chapter 10

The Eagle Crippled

 SANTA ANNA'S LATER CAREER WAS even more dramatic. He took advantage of Houston's refusal to use the firing squad to good purpose, gaining friends in Washington and political advantage in Mexico. Ensconced back on his estates after returning from Washington, his deportment continued to be a tantalizing mix of personal courage, ridiculous bravado, and mercurial rises to the heights followed by plunges into despair from which few could have recovered. Most sensational was the affair of his lost leg.

In a village not far from Mexico City a French pastrycook, who had emigrated to Mexico, operated a small but popular pâtisserie under the proud sign DULCES A LA FRANCESCA. One night a gang of drunken Mexican officers, celebrating their promotion to captain, wrecked this pastry shop, causing eight hundred pesos' worth of damage for which the owner presented a bill. The Mexican government refused to pay even that small amount and, incredible as it seemed, a war with France resulted.*

When a French fleet bombarded Veracruz, a city cherished by Santa Anna because of the many good things that had happened to him there, he leaped upon his white horse and galloped down the hill from Xalapa to defend it. This time he performed heroically. Dashing here and there to give his troops courage, he had the great good luck to be hit by an eight-pound cannonball fired by a French ship in the harbor; it damaged his left leg so seriously that it had to be amputated.

This did not deter the ambitious warrior. Promptly he had woodcarvers make him four wooden legs which he carried with him in a leather case, one for dress, one for everyday wear in the country, one for battle, and the fourth for evening wear, each different, each made of different materials. The one for evening wear was very light, made of cork.

How could the loss of a leg prove to be an

---

*The ridiculous little Pastry War of 1838 also included, of course, French demands for payment of 600,000 pesos in other claims.

act of unusual good fortune? Not only was he reinstated as president but, as one of his aides later explained:

> You'll never hear our Dictator speak four sentences in a public oration, and he makes them constantly, without hearing an account of how he lost his leg in the service of his nation. He has fifteen clever ways of casually referring to it. Heroic: "I galloped into the very mouth of the French cannon and lost my leg in doing so." Self-pity, with tears: "In a moment of great danger I surrendered my leg to the glory of my country." Challenging: "Do you think that a man who has lost his leg defending his country is afraid of a threat like that?" His missing leg ensures him the role of dictator for life. And all because of that miserable pastry shop. No man achieves greatness if he is not clever enough to use a pastry shop to his advantage, or a missing leg.

His endless apostrophes to his missing leg engendered in time a monomania regarding it, and one summer's day he invited to Manga de Clavo, his ranch at Xalapa, one of the trusted assistants into whose hands he placed government matters during the frequent periods when he resigned from the presidency. When the visitor arrived, he was astonished at the appearance of Santa Anna, extremely thin, his face poetically gaunt, his walk as he limped forward to greet his lieutenant resembling that of a cripple: 'I lost a leg, you know, defending our nation at Veracruz.' On this day he was wearing his country-landowner leg, and before his assistant could reply he reached out, clasped him by the shoulder and said with unfeigned enthusiasm: 'In honor of the great days when we defended this nation against the French, let us see the cocks fight,' and he led the way, springing along with no perceptible difficulty, to the small circular building in which he conducted his famous cockfights.

While his birds were fighting, Santa Anna revealed the astonishing duty to which the visitor had been summoned: 'Trusted companion, I seek a guard of honor for a deed of honor. In response to demands from the people of Mexico, and also its religious leaders, I have consented with some reluctance, for I am essentially a modest man, to have my left leg disinterred, borne to the capital in solemn procession, and buried in a pantheon reserved for heroes.'

'Your leg?' the visitor asked.

'Why not?' Santa Anna snapped. 'It gave itself in service to our nation. What leg has ever meant so much to any nation? Does it not deserve the treatment we give other heroes?'

'It certainly does,' the man said hurriedly, and he was present when the leg was dug up, placed upon an ornate catafalque and started on its journey to the capital.

The assistant and one of Santa Anna's young military aides designated by the dictator 'my equerry'—Santa Anna had read that English kings were served by equerries—were given specific orders: 'Leave for Mexico City right now. Ride fast and alert the town that the leg is coming. And see to it that multitudes line the avenues when it rides into town.'

Goaded by the two ambitious messengers, thousands did turn out, and at the splendid cathedral in the center of town more than fifty priests of various ranks, including a passel of bishops, waited to place the leg in a position of honor below the altar. Here legions of the faithful could come and kneel and say brief prayers.

Two days later, 28 September 1842, with Santa Anna himself in attendance, entire regiments of cavalry in resplendent uniforms, young cadets from the military academy at Chapultepec, a solemn procession of priests and religious dignitaries, the entire civilian cabinet, and most of the diplomatic corps marched to the beat of seven military bands, leaving the center of the city and progressing to the historic cemetery of Santa Paula, where a cenotaph had been erected to the dictator's leg.

Prayers were said. Chants were sung. Rifles were fired. Santa Anna wept. The multitudes cheered. And soldiers stood at reverential attention while flags were draped over the coffin and the leg lowered into its new and more stately grave.

Lamentably, the same equerry was on duty in the capital two years later when a vast revulsion against the wild pomposity of Santa Anna surfaced, and the man watched in horror as a mob tore down a gilded statue of the dictator in the center of the city, rampaged through the streets and cheered when a crazy-eyed leader shouted: 'Let's get that goddamned leg!' From a safe distance the young military man followed the frenzied rabble as it broke down the gates of Santa Paula cemetery, destroyed the cenotaph honoring the leg, dug up the bones and dragged them ignominiously through the very streets where they had previously been paraded with such majesty. He was aghast when the bones were separated, some going to one part of the city, some to another, with all of them ending in rubbish piles.

Through back streets he made his way to the palace from which the dictator had ruled with such unchallenged authority, and there he found him packing his wooden legs in their case as he prepared for flight. When the equerry informed him of events at the cemetery, the great man sat heavily upon a truck packed with silver objects and sniffled: 'My leg? The symbol of my honor? Proof of the love I hold for Mexico? You mean, they dragged it through the streets?'

With that he hobbled off to one more life-long exile, and as he disappeared in the dusk the young man mumbled: 'Mexico can never know real glory without him.'

As could have been predicted, once more Santa Anna's exile was of brief duration, but the circumstances of his return were almost incomprehensible. When conditions in Mexico deteriorated to the point of war with the United States, Mexico summoned him back and not only reinstated him as president but also conferred on him the powers of a dictator. That Mexico should invite him back was understandable, for he was a charismatic figure and to some a public hero, but that President Polk of the United States should believe reports spread by Santa Anna himself that 'if the United States helps me to return, I will be a bridge of peace between our two nations' was amazing, since Polk must have been aware of Santa Anna's mercurial switches in loyalty. When Santa Anna chartered a British steamer, however, Polk ordered U.S. naval gunboats to escort the wily Mexican back to his homeland from his exile in Havana. It was another splendid triumph, but was to have only a short life.

Determined to regain the Tejas lands lost at the Battle of San Jacinto and to punish the arrogance of the United States, this one-legged adventurer launched a huge army—as ill-equipped as ever because its officers still stole the funds intended for guns, horses and uni-

forms—into the battles taking place in what is now known as the War with Mexico of 1846. At one point it looked as if he might defeat the Americans and win back Texas, but in time superior American forces—one army pressing down from the north, a second invading through Veracruz and onto the central plateau where Mexico City itself was invaded—led to a crushing American victory and a dictated peace in which Mexico, because of the impetuous behavior of Santa Anna, surrendered huge areas of Mexican territory. Thus he became the most expensive president Mexico ever had in terms of lands lost to the nation.

Exiled once more, this time for five years in Jamaica, Santa Anna was yet again to be recalled to the presidency by a nation slow to learn its lesson. Accepting the title 'His Most Serene Highness' in 1853, he was ousted within two years by the more liberal political factions and exiled again for almost ten years. In all he did—despite his sometimes good intentions—the results he achieved were invariably disastrous to his nation.

Although he accomplished no further irreversible damage to his country during these last twenty-eight years of his life after the war with the United States, twenty-four of them spent in exile, Santa Anna continued his attempts to insert himself into Mexican politics. Isolated at St. Thomas in the Danish Virgins, he was probably not even aware that his old adversary, Sam Houston, had died. The Mexican general had fared so poorly against the Texans that he preferred to ignore them. But he could never ignore his craving for the limelight, and he was yet to perform several more dazzling switches in his loyalties.

When the full-blooded Indian hero, Benito Juárez, had been elected president in 1861 because of his promise to bring order and democracy to Mexico, Santa Anna had applauded and volunteered his enthusiastic support for the new order.

As could have been anticipated, as soon as Juárez ran into trouble, Santa Anna declared himself an enemy of the new regime. Within two years, by 1863, the conservatives opposed to Juárez were concluding bitterly that 'no Mexican is qualified to govern this nation. Our politicians are all rascals.' Santa Anna agreed, not realizing that it was also he they were condemning, and declared himself an enemy of the Juárez regime. He noisily encouraged the conservatives when they proposed a most radical solution: a desperate petition to the flamboyant Emperor of France, Napoleon III, begging him to find them a responsible European prince who would come to Mexico and serve as emperor. Complying, Napoleon made an excellent choice, the serious, capable younger brother of the Emperor of Austria.

Archduke Maximilian was thirty-one years old, tall, slim, handsome and gifted with an

above-average intelligence; of equal importance, he was married to the exquisitely
beautiful daughter of the King of Belgium.
Marie-Charlotte-Amélie-Augustine-Victoire-
Clémentine-Léopoldine would be known in
history as the fey Carlota, Empress of Mexico,
loyal wife to Emperor Maximilian.

After their triumphant entry into Mexico, it
didn't take Santa Anna long to remember he
had always been a monarchist, whereupon he
offered his support to the royal couple—until
their reign started to deteriorate. When Napoleon III failed to send troops to support the
young rulers, and when the United States made
menacing noises over Maximilian's presence
in Mexico in violation of the Monroe Doctrine,
which forbade such European intervention in
American affairs, Santa Anna swiftly abandoned the emperor. From the Virgin Islands,
where he was again in exile, he issued what he
proudly called 'my Manifesto of 8 July 1865,'
latest in line of his bombastic effusions. Of it
he boasted: 'My manifesto was extremely popular wherever it was read and helped to bring
about the revolution against Maximilian which
followed.'

His mercurial rejection of the emperor did
him no good, for he was not invited back to
head the military opposition which was growing. Instead he remained in the Virgin Islands,
a lonely, one-legged man now in his failing
seventies who stumped about St. Thomas pre-

senting a doleful figure sustained only by the fatuous dream that he might soon be recalled to lead the nation again. In this almost pathetic confusion he plunged headlong into the most preposterous of his adventures.

One January day in 1866, as he lounged in a waterfront bar regaling a group of Danish sailors with tales of the glorious days when he ruled Mexico, an American sailor ran in with exhilarating news: 'General! That ship out there! It's from America and who do you suppose is aboard? The United States Secretary of State, a man named Seward, and he's come especially to see you!'

Santa Anna rose, assumed a majestic posture, dusted off his clothes and said: 'I'm not surprised. He's come to enlist my help in throwing that interloper Maximilian out of Mexico.' Then he added, with a display of imperial dignity: 'I go to visit no one. I was head of a great nation. Let him come to see me.' He stalked off to his mean quarters to prepare as best he could to receive the American whose money would enable him, Santa Anna, to march back to Mexico at the head of an invading army of liberation.

Actually, William H. Seward, a shrewd and able politician who had served as President Lincoln's secretary of state throughout the Civil War and who now held the same position under the new president, Andrew Johnson, had sailed to St. Thomas to see if he could buy the Virgin Islands from Denmark to serve as an American naval base in the Caribbean.*

Although Seward had not come to St. Thomas to see Santa Anna, he did pay the vain old man the courtesy of coming ashore for a visit which lasted less than an hour, but even this brief contact with power so inflamed the General that he convinced himself a plot was underway to overthrow Maximilian and he, Santa Anna, was to lead it, supported by American men and money.

That night he could not sleep. When Seward's ship quietly slipped away in the morning, without leaving a promise of anything nor even a discussion of possibilities, Santa Anna did not lose heart. 'Negotiations at our level,' he explained to the waterfront sailors who watched the ship depart, 'are not conducted with bugles.'

There the harmless misunderstanding should have died, but the devious Mexican shysters who always clustered about Santa Anna saw a chance to bilk the old man of the remaining funds he had brought with him into exile; they concocted a letter, supposedly from

---

*In 1866 Seward's plan seemed visionary and nothing came of it. Disappointed, he instead bought Alaska for $7,200,00 in 1867. The Virgin Islands were not acquired by the United States until 1917, fifty-two years later, for $25,000,000.

Seward, promising huge American funds for an invasion to expel Maximilian. This money, the letter intimated, would be waiting for Santa Anna as soon as he came to New York to receive it.

The foolish old man was duped into sinking most of his remaining money into the scatter-brained purchase of an expensive ship on which he sailed hopefully to America, fully convinced that he would be using that same ship for his triumphal invasion of Mexico. Alas, when he sailed into New York he met only with disaster. He had given his conspirators the money to purchase the ship, but they had not handed the funds over to the owner. Santa Anna was technically a pirate with a stolen ship. Nor had Secretary Seward any knowledge of his coming nor any wish to discuss chimerical plans for an invasion; Santa Anna was left stranded in America without a ship or friends or money.

Despite the disasters which overwhelmed him in America, he did leave one indelible mark on that country. Always a shrewd conniver, he had brought with him on one of his trips a remarkable whitish fluid produced by the chicle tree of Yucatán. 'When you cure this liquid,' he explained to a group of New York businessmen, 'it hardens and assumes a chewy character. Then if you mix in sugar and a touch of mint, it tastes great.' American chewing gum was thus introduced to world markets thanks to the imagination of Santa Anna.

In May 1867 he heard the exciting news that Emperor Maximilian had been executed by a Juárez firing squad, and for a brief moment he hoped that a resurgent Juárez would invite him back to help govern Mexico, but his dream was futile. Juárez, aware of the fickle nature of Santa Anna's support, refused to have anything further to do with him. He would not persecute the foolish old man, but neither would he pay any attention to him. So far as Mexico was concerned, Santa Anna no longer existed. If he wished to return he was free to do so, but no drums or bugles would announce his arrival.

Fortunately he was spared knowledge of one tragic consequence of his abandonment of Maximilian and his fragile empress, Carlota. When she learned of her husband's execution, the shock was so great that she drifted into a hopeless insanity. Outliving all the other participants in these turbulent years of victory and despair, she returned to a chateau in Belgium where she existed for sixty more years as a wild-eyed lunatic until 1927.

In 1874, in his eightieth year, Santa Anna lived as a forlorn exile, the 'Wandering Jew' of Mexican politics, in Nassau in the Bahamas where he penned the last pages of his autobiography, a melange of both bitter accusations against all who had treated him badly and pathetic explanations as to why certain actions which might have looked disgraceful at the time had really been dictated by the highest moral principles and by his meticulous adherence to the code of honor. Ridiculous as these self-serving justifications were, occasional passages could be either deeply moving or bewildering in their contradiction of fact.

For eighteen years and six months I have endured a heartrending exile from my native land. My political enemies have pursued me relentlessly, heaping insults on my head. Nothing is sacred to them. They have drained me dry. They have wrenched from me all that I gained during the many years of sacrifices by my sweat and blood. They have left me without a parcel of land, without a hut to shelter my bones, without a stone to lay my head on . . .

When I close my eyes forever, I wish to be judged merely as I am, not as my enemies would have me be. If I were to ask for a title, it would merely be that of "Patriot." I leave to the understanding and conscientious reader to examine all the facts and draw his own conclusions as to my trustworthiness. . . .

All who are burdened with the reading of my Memoirs, must surely see in my deeds only a patriot serving his nation to the best of his ability. I am confident that I will be worthy of my country's gratitude, and I have even

greater confidence that posterity will
do me full justice.

To the end of his days, even in his near-blind
eighties, Santa Anna never ceased his machi-
nations to recover his lost glory. An opportunity for one final scheming hoax occurred
when, in 1876 during his last year in office,
President Ulysses S. Grant, eager to improve
relations with his neighboring republic, dispatched a secret emissary to Mexico City to
negotiate a trade agreement. For this delicate
assignment he chose a trusted veteran who
had fought beside him at the great Siege of
Vicksburg, losing an arm in defense of a Union
redoubt. Traveling incognito as a Mr. Bascomb, this gentleman set sail with his wife for
Mexico.

When they disembarked at Veracruz and
boarded the waiting train that would carry
them to Mexico City, they had barely reached
their seats in the parlor car when an ebullient
Mexican gentleman approached, eager to help
make their journey enjoyable. 'Look at that
old fortress in the bay. Half the famous men in
our history cringed in its cells.'

Shivering, he continued: 'Did you know that
your Santa Anna was in one of them for a
while?'

'Why did you say "My Santa Anna"?'

'Well, you bought him, didn't you? You paid
him to do the dreadful things he did to us Mexicans, didn't you?'

'I know him only as a name,' the emissary replied. 'I'm Texan, you know, and our children hear rumors about what Santa Anna did to us.'

'Were you born in Texas?'

'South Carolina.'

'See!' the Mexican cried triumphantly. 'Your government sent thousands of people from the states. To steal Texas from us.'

'I came long after that,' Bascomb said.

'Most curious,' the Mexican said in Spanish. 'Never do I meet anyone who was born in Texas. You all crept in as thieves.'

'Did Santa Anna die behind those prison walls?'

'He didn't die. He's living in Mexico City right now. Near my sister.'

'The great Santa Anna? Of the Alamo? You mean he's still alive?'

'One leg and all. Many times exiled, supposedly for life. Always invited back. Last time he was living in Cuba or Nassau or maybe the Danish Virgins. He lived everywhere. But always he limped home.'

'I can't believe this. He must be nearly ninety.'

'He's old, no titles, no land, no money, but he's as alive as you or me. At least he was when I sailed for New Orleans.'

Bascomb made a pact with the businessman: 'When we reach Mexico City you must take me to see your old hero.'

'I'll take you to my sister. She knows where he lives.'

As the train made the tortuous climb up to the *altoplano* on which Mexico City perched among its volcanos, the Mexican said brightly: 'Mr. Bascomb, you haven't told me why you're here.'

'To achieve a lasting peace between our two nations.'

At this startling news the Mexican fell silent, then broke into a congenial laugh: 'Peace! You Americans have done everything to make peace impossible. Invaded us. Stolen our lands. Bought our president. Humiliated us.' He threw up his hands and roared: 'But here we still are, Mexico down here, you bumping against us up there. Nothing on earth will ever separate us, so I suppose you're right. We'd better make some kind of peace.'

Bascomb did not expect to hear from the man again, but on the third day at the embassy he appeared: 'I've brought my sister, and she'll take you to Santa Anna.' Threading her way through the poor section of the city, the woman led the way to a mean, crowded street in which Generalísimo Santa Anna, once the owner of four million acres, lived in obscure poverty.

'He'll be in here,' the woman said as she knocked on the rough wooden door. 'A visitor from the United States' she told Señora Santa Anna, garbed in black with few vestiges of the pert beauty the General had married after the death of his wife. She escorted the visitors into the first of the two small rooms, then disappeared into the inner room.

In the pause that followed Bascomb surveyed the quarters: four differently clad wooden legs hanging from a rack; desk piled high with yellowing papers; three chairs with their cane seats damaged; a chromolithograph of the great man astride a horse in his days of glory.

The beaded curtain separating the two rooms parted and an old man of eighty-two, noticeably tall for a Mexican, hopped in on one leg. His gaze was vacant, his teeth stained, and his speech faltering as he welcomed his visitor, but his hair was still that ebon black.

When the guide introduced Bascomb as 'an ambassador from the United States,' the old warrior's bearing stiffened, his visage hardened and he became a general once more, president of a sovereign state.

'You must excuse me,' he apologized in Spanish. Then in good English he added: 'I've been working on my memoirs.' With that he hopped to the wall, took down his dress leg and affixed it to his left stump, after which he walked over to Bascomb and shook his hand warmly: 'I am always eager to consult with plenipotentiaries from our sister republic to the north.' In a long report to President Grant, his secret emissary explained what happened next:

The poor old fellow conceived the notion that you had sent me to arrange some kind of treaty with him, whereby he would lead Mexico into a permanent relationship with our country, and before I could disabuse him he rattled off like a rapidly firing musket several proposals, one of which he felt sure must interest you. Each suggested plan of action started with our government depositing three million of our dollars to his account. With this he would persuade his government, in which he assured me he still played a leading role, to make conciliatory gestures. He was certain that with three million dollars, properly applied, he could effect permanent peace between our nations.

When I started to explain the limited nature of my visit with him, namely that I wanted to pay my respects to a general so famous in Texas history, he concluded that I had found his first offer too expensive, so he said with growing excitement: 'Mr. Ambassador, I assure you that for a mere two million dollars I could arrange a most spectacular treaty between my country and yours,' and now he proposed two other lines of operation completely at variance with the one first suggested.

At one point he peered at me closely, trying to discern my face through his near-total blindness, and he concluded that I was Secretary of State Seward come to seek his help in overthrowing Emperor Maximilian. He advanced several visionary suggestions as to how we might accomplish this, but when I reminded him that Maximilian was long gone he sighed: 'Of course. The beast Juárez shot him. Shameful. But Seward, my friend, such acts do happen in Mexico and we men of honor deplore them.'

I finally had to tell him, rather bluntly I'm afraid, that I had come solely to pay my respects to him as an old warrior and nothing more, and I could see his shoulders sag and the fire leave his face. 'I am a worn-out old man,' he told me almost pathetically. 'See what they've done to my estates,' and he fumbled among his papers. Aware that he could not see me, I looked more closely and detected a heavy film across his eyes.

He told me that during his most recent banishment for life, on November 1, 1867, for his memory about his own affairs was exceptional, the government had confiscated all his estates, those vast holdings in the Veracruz area,

199

and he was now forced to live on the charity of friends. 'But I have many friends,' he assured me, 'and if your government said only one word of encouragement, they would call me back to the presidency.' He added with obvious pride: 'I've been president eleven times, you know, always at the insistence of the people.'

When he said this he reached out to take my arm, for although he could apparently make out large forms he could not see clearly enough to know that I had lost my left arm. As he fumbled for it he suddenly stopped and said: 'Secretary Seward! I apprehend that you have lost your arm. In battle I hope?'

'Vicksburg,' I said, and on the spur of the moment he uttered a critique of that affair in which you played so notable a role, and he astonished me with the depth of his knowledge, for names rolled off his lively tongue with the greatest of ease, and not once did he make an error.

As he completed his military analysis he cried with sparkling enthusiasm 'Inform your president that by his gallant performance at Vicksburg he won the admiration of the Napoleon of the West.'

When he perceived that I was about to leave he begged me to stay, so I humored him, and this gave him renewed courage, for with great excitement he outlined what I had to admit was a most sensible plan, under the circumstances. For a mere million dollars deposited to his account he would undertake to persuade the Mexican government to enter an agreement which would endure as long as the Rio Grande separated our two countries. When I said that I must depart, he accompanied me into the street, walking boldly and without a sign of limp. Children running past paused to shout 'Hello, General' but they did not stop.

At the end he saluted, smartly, and begged me to return for he had several other proposals which he felt sure would interest you. Some weeks later he was dead, and I was one of a handful who followed his mean cortege to the pauper's corner of the graveyard where he was buried. At his insistence, his four legs were buried with him.

While Bascomb and his wife were walking home from the funeral, he fell into a contemplative mood: 'Santa Anna and Houston, you cannot think of one without judging the other. Alike in so many ways . . . wonderful triumphs, soul-shattering defeats. They occupied all the positions of power ... General, Senator, President, Dictator. But both suffered exile and died in disgrace.'

It was Mrs. Bascomb who delivered the funeral oration for the two heroes: 'They were both patriots, each in his own stubborn way.'

Chapter 11

Birds of Different Feathers

 EAGLE AND RAVEN! HOW similar the two men were: egotistical, brave beyond ordinary standards, lovers of battle and gunsmoke, ambitious, moody, not afraid to withdraw to solitude for a regrouping of their ideas, taller than their companions, more clever, quick to make decisions, and each convinced that he operated under a star of good fortune.

Each had known extraordinary success. Each had attained the rank of general, on merit, and each had been supreme executive of the area in which he labored. By 1836 Santa Anna had perfected his irresponsible trick of skipping in and out of the presidency, while Houston was engaged in what would be his more disciplined progress: congressman and governor of Tennessee, president of the new nation of Texas, United States senator and governor of the new state of Texas. Each had stepped down from high office by choice and gone into his chosen retreat to regroup his forces and plans. And each loved the high drama of life, the flamboyant gesture that bespoke the adventurer.

One of the most intriguing similarities between the two men involved their relationships with women. Each had contracted his first marriage relatively late, Santa Anna to a reclusive woman who served him in silence, Houston to a young neurotic who nearly destroyed his life. But each found a second wife preposterously younger than himself who brought great joy. Houston chose a sedate clergyman's daughter who bore him many fine children, but Santa Anna, as would be expected, followed a more dramatic course.

When his wonderfully stable first wife died in 1844, Santa Anna paraded before the public a moving display of grief, but for only two months, after which he grabbed a beautiful fifteen-year-old girl of extraordinary beauty. Their marriage outraged the stabler elements of Mexican society, but only briefly, for the new wife proved a saucy lass who ingratiated herself with everyone. Quickly she showed that she did not intend hiding herself away at the ranch in Xalapa as the first wife had done; she preferred the gay activity of the capital with its dancing and flirting. Older women who watched her in the first months of her marriage predicted: 'That one isn't going to stay married to a one-legged man old enough to be her grandfather. She'll drop him in a hurry if things go bad, and with Santa Anna they always do.' But they were wrong.

This captivating young woman who could have run off with almost any man she wanted, proved amazingly loyal to her tarnished hero. Even when the last of his grandiose dreams evaporated and he was in his failing eighties, she was still there, sharing with him a near hovel. Neighbors heard them brawling now and then but she stayed with him, for Santa Anna inspired loyalty in his followers.

There were differences between the two generals. Santa Anna had amassed—and lost—a tremendous personal fortune; Sam Houston never had much. The Mexican had two vast estates; Houston sometimes had little more than a dog-trot cabin. Houston had fought duels to defend his honor; Santa Anna had his own elastic definitions of that word.

In their attitudes toward religion both men, although ostensibly adherent to their different faiths, were capable of sacrificing belief to prudence. Houston, a Protestant but one who had been denied membership in his church and who had to remain unbaptized until late in life, nominally converted to Catholicism for a short time in order to qualify for land grants under Mexican laws. Santa Anna, the Catholic, had attained the presidency by joining the liberal fight against the church's privileges, but as an older man he once again became a fanatical defender of those ancient rights, perhaps to gain political and financial advantage. When he wished to declare war on the rebels in Tejas and found his treasury bankrupt, he once more turned to the church, whose bishops lent him at no interest, or gave him outright, huge sums for his campaign.

The two also differed in their approach to slavery, and in ways that could not have been anticipated. Houston, the man who fought for freedom, also defended the right of his fellow Americans to own slaves in Tejas. Santa Anna, a man who had repeatedly crushed even the slightest manifestation of men seeking political freedom, honestly adopted his government's position of vigorous opposition to slavery. Indeed he seemed proud of the fact that Mexico in 1829 had been the first nation in the New World to bar slavery, thirty-four years before the United States had the courage to do so in 1863. One of the gravest charges the Tejas Americans advanced against him was that 'he's comin' north to take away our slaves.' This was true. Mexico had witnessed centuries of cruel enslavement of its Indians by harsh Spanish masters and was determined to tolerate no more. Of course, this public posture concealed considerable private cynicism, for hidden slavery was rampant in the rural and mining areas of Mexico and would continue into the next century.

At any rate, Santa Anna intended to enforce the edict outlawing slavery, but from the Americans he received only obloquy for this intention. According to their reasoning his action, which might have been interpreted as a protection of freedom for the black man, was really a blow against the freedoms of the white. They argued fiercely that in threatening to deprive them of their slaves, Santa Anna proved himself an enemy of human freedom, and they were prepared to die to protect that freedom.

Now, a fascinating question arises: Did either of these two adversaries know much about the other? Historians can only speculate. Houston must have known a good deal about Santa Anna's personality and behavior in both politics and battle; he was president of the nation in which Houston had lived for some time, and his actions had been widely discussed and analyzed. On the other hand, it is possible that Santa Anna did not even know of Sam Houston's existence. Perhaps he had heard his name mentioned as merely one more of that troublesome breed of newcomers onto Mexican soil: Jim Bowie, Davy Crockett, William Travis, James Fannin, Sam Houston. He would defeat and discipline them all . . . by firing squad or hanging.

An amusing similarity: Each man, markedly more handsome than his colleagues, loved ornate, or at least unusual, dress. Santa Anna adored the ultra-expensive military uniform bedecked with medals and gold trim; Sam Houston could never be persuaded to dress like ordinary men. At the most improper times, such as a meeting at the White House, he would appear in the wildest Indian costume. When distinguished visitors like the Frenchman de Tocqueville met him, he was apt to appear with almost no clothes, his hair uncombed, his face unshaved, smelly, dirty, obnoxious. Another time he might step forward in gorgeous furs and wearing ornamental metal disks suspended from his neck, with a huge oaken stave in his left hand as if he were an emperor. When asked to sit for his portrait as governor of Tennessee he appeared naked except for a Roman toga thrown carelessly about his shoulders, and was so painted.

A sobering difference: As a political leader Sam Houston lived to witness the final victory in almost everything he attempted. As a young man he was a responsible United States congressman and a stalwart governor of Tennessee. Later he played a crucial role in establishing the sovereign nation of Texas, served with distinction as its president, and was instrumental in bringing it into the United States, which he served as an able senator. Even in the darkest days of the Civil War, when he was thrown from office because he refused to fight for the Confederacy, he made the sensible choice, for he knew the North must win. He was a stubborn man, convinced that he must prevail if he did things his own way. He left everything he touched somewhat better than it had been when he assumed responsibility for it.

As a military man, General Santa Anna enjoyed such great success at the beginning of his career that it was not foolish for his subordinates to indulge him by using his self-created title, The Napoleon of the West. But in his two major battles, San Jacinto in 1836 and the war with the United States ten years later, he suffered catastrophic defeats, largely because of his own inadequate generalship. In the civil government of Mexico, where he enjoyed dictatorial powers, he could have engineered his nation's move into the modern world but, lacking any sense of what democracy really was, or even any well-defined central platform of his own, he oscillated like a wobbling top come to the end of its spin. Most damaging, he could never prove faithful to decisions he himself had made. Because of his almost pathetic exhibitions of a personal and confused leadership, when he finally departed the national scene he left Mexico infinitely worse off than it had been when he assumed control.

And finally a devastating contrast: Sam Houston utilized his various presidencies and governorships as an opportunity to enhance

the dignity of those offices. His impeccable deportment helped create the unique and favorable reputation that Texas gained among the
states, and he is now enthroned in Texas
hearts. Santa Anna, on the other hand, used
the Mexican presidency to satisfy his ambitions, prancing in and out of office as his
vanity dictated. He trivialized what could
have been a majestic office, leaving it weak-
ened and debased. He did not even protect it,
as a leader should, and Mexicans today cannot
forgive him for having been the instrument
whereby their country lost such vast areas of
land to the United States: Texas, New Mexico,
Arizona, southern California, and even lands
to the north of these now rich and prosperous
states. As a political leader he was not only a
disaster, but, what was worse, an embarrassment. This explains why there is in Mexico today no grand national monument honoring
him, even though he was the dominant figure
of his era. Mexicans try to forget him.

Eagle and Raven! They were not ordinary
men, and never in their long lives did they be-
have in ordinary ways. Similar in much, they
differed in one crucial dimension. Houston
had a heart of oak, forever loyal to the principles to which he had been bred and upon
which he had nurtured during his embattled
career. Santa Anna was a bending willow, subservient to every storm, elegant and daring,
but never faithful to any principle, not even

those of his own devising. A national leader may accumulate a spectacular chain of temporary results, but unless his character has been forged in the fires of integrity and his actions in the crucible of hard-edged reason, history will refuse to stamp him with the seal of greatness.

Appendix 1:
Letters Mentioned in the Book

Letter from Sam Houston to James Prentis,
April 20, 1834

Washington City, 20th Ap¹ 1834

Dear Sir, I hourly expect a letter from you inclosing my Map—In answer to your last request I will assure you, that I will not omit to attend to your individual interest, and that of your Brother. You doubtless saw the extract contained in the Intelligencer of some day last week. I don't recollect what day, but you can find it.

Now as to Texas, I will give you my candid impressions—I do not think that it will be acquired by the U States. I do think within one year that it will be a Sovreign State and acting in all things as such. Within three years I think it will be separated from the Mexican Confedracy, and remain so forever—

Letters from Co¹ Butler state that every thing is unsettled in Mexico and that Revolution is going on— Gen¹ Bravo, and others are in the field— Success is not certain on either side— Gen¹ Santa Ana is absent, and the Vice President Administers the Government. I assure you Santa Ana aspires to the *Purple*, and should he assume it, you know Texas is off from them and so to remain—

You may reflect upon these suggestions— They are not pleasant to me, but you may file them, and see how well I *prophesy*—Write to me directly, as I must set out on Thursday for the West. Should I have left here, my letters will be forwarded to me by a friend

Houston

To Mr. James Prentiss

[Addressed]: Mr. James Prentiss   Wall Street   New York   Mail.

[Endorsed]: Genl Saml Houston   20th April   1834

Facsimile of Sam Houston's letter to James Prentis, April 20, 1834

Source: the Sam Houston Papers, Barker Texas History Center, the University of Texas at Austin.

the Mexican confederacy, and union
Is forever—

Letters from Col Butler state
that every thing is unsettled in Mexico
and that Revolution is going on— Genl
Bravo and others are in the field— Success
is not certain on either side— Genl
San ta Ana is absent, and the Vice
President administers the Government

I assure you Santa Ana aspires
to the Purple, and should he assume
it, you know Texas is off from them
and is to America—

You may reflect upon these
suggestions— They are not pleasant to
me, but you may file them, and
see how well I prophesy— Write
to me directly, as I must set out

on Thursday for the West — Should
I have left here, my letters will
be forwarded to my by a friend
Truly yours
in hast
Houston

To Mr James Prentiss

*Letter from Sam Houston to James Prentis,
April 24, 1834*

Washington City   24th Apl   1834

My dear Sir, I received your favors, and the Map sent by your son, but had not the pleasure to see him. I intend to call, and see him before I leave here, as I wish to become acquainted with him.

I thank you for what you have done, and the solicitude, which you entertain for my interest— It is *all* right, for take my word for it, *they* will *need* me more than I will *want* them!

I have written to you just my *opinions*, on the course which things, must, and will take in Texas. She cannot, and will not remain as she now is. Keep my predictions, and see how far they are *verified!*

I do not know what "important Political movements" they are to which you allude, and as I may, be detained here for some days, I want you to let me know what they are!

You need not hope for the acquisition (if ever) by this Government of Texas during the Administration of Genl Jackson—If it were acquired by a Treaty, that Treaty, would not be ratified, by the present Senate—!!!

Texas, will be bound to look to herself, and to do for herself—This present year, must produce events, important to her future destiny. *I think*, greatly beneficial to her prosperity. I depricate the necessity,—and however favorable the result, may be for her— Still if Mexico had done right, we cou'd have travelled on smoothly enough.

Many suppose that such events will, be sought for by us, but in this their notions will be gratuitous, I assure you! The course that I may pursue, you must rely upon it, shall be for the true interests of Texas, (as I may believe) and if it can be done, as it ought to be; to preserve her integrity to the Confederacy of Mexico.

Sam Houston

Mr. James Prentiss

P.S. Write directly to me, and enclose to Mr. Grundy; or the Hon'ble Ratcliff Boon Member of Congress.

[Addressed]: To Mr. James Prentiss Wall Street New York
[Endorsed]: Genl Sam; Houston 24 April 1834.

Facsimile of Sam Houston's letter to James Prentis, April 24, 1834

Source: the Sam Houston Papers, Barker Texas History Center, the University of Texas at Austin.

keep my predictions, and see how
far they are verified.'

"I do not know to what
important political movements" they
they are, to which you allude, and
as I may, be detained here for
some days, I want you to let
me know what they are.'

(You must not hope for
for the acquisition (if ever) by
the Government of Texas during the administration of Genl Jackson. If
it were acquired by a Treaty, the
Treaty, would not be ratified, by
the present Senate.."

Texas, will be bound to look
to herself, and to do for herself-
this present year, must produce
events, important, to her future

Letter from William Travis to the People of Texas, February 24, 1836

Commandancy of the Alamo-Bejar,
Feby. 24th, 1836

To the People of Texas & all Americans in the world—

Fellow citizens & compatriots—

I am beseiged, by a thousand or more of the Mexicans under Santa Anna—I have sustained a continual Bombardment & cannonade for 24 hours & have not lost a man—The enemy has demanded a surrender at discretion otherwise the garrison are to be put to the sword, if the fort is taken—I have answered the demand with a cannon shot, & our flag still waves proudly from the walls—*I shall never surrender or retreat. Then*, I call on you in the name of Liberty, of patriotism & everything dear to the American character, to come to our aid, with all dispatch—The enemy is receiving reinforcements daily & will no doubt increase to three or four thousand in four or five days. If this call is neglected, I am determined to sustain myself as long as possible & die like a soldier who never forgets what is due to his own honor & that of his country—VICTORY OR DEATH.

William Barret Travis,
Lt. Col. comdt.

P.S. The Lord is on our side—When the enemy appeared in sight we had not three bushels of corn—We have since found in deserted houses 80 or 90 bushels and got into the walls 20 or 30 head of Beeves—

Travis

The Eagle and The Raven

Facsimile of the original letter from William Travis to the People of Texas and all Americans in the world, February 24, 1836.

Source: The Texas State Archives

... in ill dispatch — the enemy is receiving reinforcements daily & will no doubt increase to three or four thousand in four or five days. If this call is neglected, I am determined to sustain myself as long as possible & die like a soldier who never forgets what is due to his own honor & that of his country —

Victory or Death

William Barret Travis
Lt. Col. comdt.

*P.S. ...
When the enemy appeared in sight we had not three bushels of corn — we have since found in deserted houses 80 or 90 bushels & got into the walls 20 or 30 head of Beeves —*

Travis

Appendix 2:
Chronology

SANTA ANNA		SAM HOUSTON
	1793	Birth
Birth	1794	
Cavalry officer	1812	Opens school
Battle of Medina	1813	Joins the army
	1823	House of Representatives
Retirement at Manga Clavo	1827	Governor of Tennessee
Tampico	1829	1st marriage and separation
1st Presidency	1833	Constitutional Convention
Rape of Zacatecas	1835	
Campaigns in Texas	1836	Head of Tejas army
SAN JACINTO	**1836**	**SAN JACINTO**
Goes to Washington	1836	1st President of Texas
Loses leg in Pastry War	1838	
2d Presidency	1839	Texas Legislature
	1840	2nd marriage
3d Presidency	1841	3rd President of Texas
Burial of leg	1842	
2d marriage	1844	Campaigns for U.S. statehood

Exiled for life/Cuba	1845	Texas admitted to the Union
4th Presidency/U.S. War	1846	United States Senator
Exiled for life/ Jamaica	1848	
5th Presidency/ dictator	1853	
Exiled for life/ Colombia	1855	Leader in U.S. Senate
Exiled in Virgin Islands	1859	Governor of Texas
	1861	Loses governorship
Emperor Maximilian	1863	Death
Returns to Mexico/ exiled	1864	
Seward's visit	1866	
Exiled/Nassau	1867	
Returns to Mexico	1874	
Death	1876	

Appendix 3:
Suggested Reading

Among the scores of studies consulted during the eight years this manuscript was in preparation, several works are to be especially recommended to readers of this finished book. They have been selected for two reasons: they are well written and interesting, and they can probably be found in public or college libraries. The first group comprises those used in the 1982 period.

Calcott, Wilfrid H. *Santa Anna: The Story of an Enigma Who Once Was Mexico*. 1936.

Casteñeda, Carlos E., ed. *The Mexican Side of the Texas Revolution*. 1927.

Crawford, Ann Fears, ed. *The Eagle: The Autobiography of Santa Anna*. 1967.

Friend, Llerena. *Sam Houston: The Great Designer*. 1954.

James, Marquis. *The Raven: A Biography of Sam Houston*. 1929.

Lord, Walter. *A Time to Stand*. 1961.

Tinkle, Lon. *Thirteen Days to Glory*. 1958.

Tolbert, Frank X. *The Day of San Jacinto*. 1959.

Webb, Walter Prescott, et al. *The Handbook of Texas*. Vol. I–II, 1952, Vol. III, 1976. (Forthcoming six volume set, 1995).

The second group comprises recent and forthcoming publications of exceptional relevance.

Crook, Elizabeth. *Raven's Bride*. 1991.

De Bruhl, Marshall, (untitled biography of Sam Houston to be released in 1992)

Long, Jeff. *Duel of Eagles: The Mexican and U.S. Fight for the Alamo*. 1990.

BESTSELLERS
FROM TOR

☐ ☐	50570-0	**ALL ABOUT WOMEN** Andrew M. Greeley	$4.95 Canada $5.95
☐ ☐	58341-8 58342-6	**ANGEL FIRE** Andrew M. Greeley	$4.95 Canada $5.95
☐ ☐	52725-9 52726-7	**BLACK WIND** F. Paul Wilson	$4.95 Canada $5.95
☐ ☐	51392-4	**LONG RIDE HOME** W. Michael Gear	$4.95 Canada $5.95
☐ ☐	50350-3	**OKTOBER** Stephen Gallagher	$4.95 Canada $5.95
☐ ☐	50857-2	**THE RANSOM OF BLACK STEALTH One** Dean Ing	$5.95 Canada $6.95
☐ ☐	50088-1	**SAND IN THE WIND** Kathleen O'Neal Gear	$4.50 Canada $5.50
☐ ☐	51878-0	**SANDMAN** Linda Crockett	$4.95 Canada $5.95
☐ ☐	50214-0 50215-9	**THE SCHOLARS OF NIGHT** John M. Ford	$4.95 Canada $5.95
☐ ☐	51826-8	**TENDER PREY** Julia Grice	$4.95 Canada $5.95
☐ ☐	52188-4	**TIME AND CHANCE** Alan Brennert	$4.95 Canada $5.95

Buy them at your local bookstore or use this handy coupon:
Clip and mail this page with your order.

Publishers Book and Audio Mailing Service
P.O. Box 120159, Staten Island, NY 10312-0004

Please send me the book(s) I have checked above. I am enclosing $ _____
(please add $1.25 for the first book, and $.25 for each additional book to cover postage and handling.
Send check or money order only—no CODs).

Name _____

Address _____

City _____ State/Zip _____

Please allow six weeks for delivery. Prices subject to change without notice.

WESTERN ADVENTURE
FROM TOR

☐	58459-7	THE BAREFOOT BRIGADE	$4.50
☐	58460-0	*Douglas Jones*	Canada $5.50
☐	58150-4	BETWEEN THE WORLDS (Snowblind Moon Part I)	$3.95
☐	58151-2	*John Byrne Cooke*	Canada $4.95
☐	58991-2	THE CAPTIVES	$4.50
☐	58992-0	*Don Wright*	Canada $5.50
☐	58548-8	CONFLICT OF INTEREST	$3.95
☐		*Donald McRae*	Canada $4.95
☐	58457-0	ELKHORN TAVERN	$4.50
☐	58458-9	*Douglas Jones*	Canada $5.50
☐	58453-8	GONE THE DREAMS AND DANCING	$3.95
☐	58454-6	*Douglas Jones*	Canada $4.95
☐	58154-7	HOOP OF THE NATION (Snowblind Moon Part III)	$3.95
☐	58155-5	*John Byrne Cooke*	Canada $4.95
☐	58152-0	THE PIPE CARRIERS (Snowblind Moon Part II)	$3.95
☐	58153-9	*John Byrne Cooke*	Canada $4.95
☐	58455-4	ROMAN	$4.95
☐	58456-2	*Douglas Jones*	Canada $5.95
☐	58463-5	WEEDY ROUGH	$4.95
☐	58464-3	*Douglas Jones*	Canada $5.95
☐	58989-0	WOODSMAN	$3.95
☐	58990-4	*Don Wright*	Canada $4.95

Buy them at your local bookstore or use this handy coupon:
Clip and mail this page with your order.

Publishers Book and Audio Mailing Service
P.O. Box 120159, Staten Island, NY 10312-0004

Please send me the book(s) I have checked above. I am enclosing $ _____
(please add $1.25 for the first book, and $.25 for each additional book to cover postage and handling.
Send check or money order only—no CODs).

Name _____
Address _____
City _____ State/Zip _____
Please allow six weeks for delivery. Prices subject to change without notice.

SKYE'S WEST
BY RICHARD S. WHEELER

The thrilling saga of a man and the vast Montana wilderness...
SKYE'S WEST
by the author of the 1989 Spur Award-Winning novel *Fool's Coach*

"Among the new wave of western writers, Richard S. Wheeler is a standout
performer."
—*El Paso Herald-Post*